MY ARROGANT BOSS

KYLIE KING

ABOUT MY ARROGANT BOSS

The guy I hate the most is now my new boss…

Finn Weston is CEO of one of the hottest companies around and he's every girls' dream guy—every girl *except* me.

Ever since the day I tossed my champagne in his face at my best friend's party, we've never gotten along. But, hey, it wasn't like he didn't deserve it.

After losing my job and being left with no choice but to find another, I came to the awful realization that my new position was to work for the infamous jerk, Finn.

I've despised this guy for months, even though he has the body of a god and a smile to die for—and, sure, he's really easy on the eyes and there are moments when I want to climb him like a tree—but still, I loathe everything about him.

Finn has made it his mission to show me who's really in charge, but in doing so we're left with no choice but to get closer. And one night in a hotel is all it takes for my irritatingly hot boss to not seem so irritating to me anymore...

CHAPTER ONE

FINN

"Oh, wait! Turn here!" my best friend Aaron shouted from the passenger seat. The tires of my Range Rover screeched as I took a sudden short turn onto a car-packed street.

"You know what? Maybe you should've driven," I grumbled, gripping the steering wheel.

"Like hell you would've agreed to that," he countered.

I laughed. He had a point. I didn't like riding with anyone. I preferred to be the driver, and perhaps that stemmed from my need for control in all aspects of my life, but I didn't care. I probably would've offered no complaints to him if my nerves hadn't been on edge since that morning. I wasn't up for the night planned, but Aaron was my best friend, and I couldn't deny him my presence for his special event.

I could see the house we were to visit down the road, one side of it lined with parked cars. My fingers gripped the steering wheel as I found a spot to squeeze into a block away.

"I still don't think this is a good idea," I said, sighing as I put the car in Park.

"It'll be fine. Just chill." Aaron capped my shoulder before stepping out of the car. By the time I unfastened my seatbelt and stepped out of the car, Aaron was already standing by the front of it, waiting impatiently as he stared at the front of the house that had an elegant white awning above the entrance door.

He turned to me and, sensing my reluctant mood, and said, "Look, as long as you keep to yourself, tonight will be fine. Rachel is hosting for Katie, and you know Katie needs me here tonight, and I'd hate having this night without you. After all, you *are* my best man."

"Best man," I scoffed. The title didn't suit me. And it said a lot about Aaron because *best man* were two words a person would never use to describe me as a man. There was a person waiting inside that house, and I knew she wanted to call me all sorts of derogatory names. Jackass. Asshole. Shithead. The list went on.

I didn't want to go in there and deal with the glaring daggers she was ready to throw at me. I wanted to take the first flight back to California and put the biggest gap ever between me and Rachel Quinn. The way we first met was far from pleasant and resulted in her throwing a flute of champagne in my face. Of course, I deserved it. I was a jerk to her that day and took my irritations out on her.

Now, I was standing outside the sleek house where she was hosting an engagement party for Aaron and Katie, to whom she would be playing bridesmaid to the day of the wedding.

I followed after Aaron in my three-piece suit, adjusting my collar and preparing for the worst. The music amplified the closer we got to the house, and Aaron suddenly pulled me to the side. "Seriously, I know I've said it many times, but you don't have to like Rachel, alright? All you have to do is pretend to get along for the sake of the wedding."

What a load of bullshit. I wasn't the type to "get along" with people I didn't want to be friends with.

On the Finn Weston scale, other people's views of me meant nothing. Aaron, who I'd known since high school, knew that about me, but he also knew I wouldn't make an ass out of myself during *his* engagement party.

Aaron walked ahead again. "And if you can't say anything nice to or about her, don't say anything at all," he added for good measure.

"Yeah, yeah. I got it." I would have had to have been speechless for the rest of my life if I followed through with that.

I couldn't say anything good about her because I couldn't allow myself to consider anything was nice about her. For fucks sake, I struggled to look the woman in the eyes because all I felt was a burning resentment for her. Yes, it was *that* deep. I'd never been so humiliated by a woman in my life until I met her.

We approached the door, and I braced myself. Aaron pulled at the handle to open it, and as soon as we walked in, there she was.

CHAPTER TWO

FINN

Standing in a purple cocktail dress with amber eyes and a bright, wide smile directed at Aaron was my nightmare.

Rachel fucking Quinn.

I clenched my jaw as Aaron greeted her and watched as she acknowledged him with a big smile, her eyes twinkling beneath the crystal chandelier above her.

"Hi, Aaron! You look so handsome!" she said, still smiling.

"Oh, stop it," Aaron grinned, teasing. "You look

absolutely radiant, Rachel. Seriously, how do you do it?"

"Oh, stop it." Rachel giggled and hugged Aaron around the shoulders. "So good to see you."

As she pulled away, her eyes shifted up to mine, and as if she knew this time was coming, I noticed her nostrils flare, but she forced a smile at me anyway. "Finn," she said, nodding.

"Rachel."

God, she was beautiful. That was more so the reason I couldn't stand her. Her beauty was the first thing I noticed about her, but she'd caught me at a bad time when we first met, and I'd given myself very little time to embrace that. Now, hell would have to freeze over before I gave her any sort of compliment on her looks. I wasn't Aaron. I could easily pretend I didn't notice.

"Aaron, I'll need your keys," she said, directing her to Aaron again, deliberately avoiding having to look at me. "It's the rules for tonight. We don't want anyone drunk at the wheel, so we're monitoring before handing keys back when the guests are ready to go, and seeing as we have some guests here who are known to be *ignorant* and *careless*," she spat, "we have to do what's best."

That last part was for me, and she made that

perfectly clear by cutting her eyes at me and narrowing them before focusing on Aaron again and sticking her hand out.

"Oh, well, the keys are with Finn," Aaron said as he stepped past her, distracted. "I didn't drive." Katie was down the hallway, and he abandoned the conversation, rushing away to meet up with his fiancée, picking her up, and giving her a kiss.

Rachel sighed. Now she had no choice but to look at me, and a part of me wanted to gloat and laugh in her face about it.

"I'll need your keys, Finn," she said.

I folded my arms. "What if I don't want to give them to you?"

"Then you'll have to leave now. Those are the rules, and just because you're Aaron's best man doesn't mean you get to change them. We'll have drinking games, and we have to monitor all drivers for safety." She stuck her hand out impatiently. "So, if you want in and don't want to ruin one of the biggest highlights of your best friend's life, I'll need your keys. *Now*."

Her voice indicated she was done arguing with me.

"You know what?" I dug into my pocket. "I refuse to argue with you tonight or at any given time during Aaron and Katie's celebrations." I dropped the keys into her open palm.

Rachel gave me a smug smile. "See how easy that was? Thank you, Finn." Sarcasm dripped with every word of hers. "Now you can go in and enjoy your night."

I strode briskly past Rachel and toward the main ballroom, and if I weren't mistaken, I heard a small laugh when I was halfway down the hallway. I really couldn't stand her, and though I said I wouldn't argue, I knew she was going to make it hard as hell to keep my mouth shut and be the bigger person.

She couldn't stand me. And that was totally fine because I couldn't stand her ass either.

CHAPTER THREE

RACHEL

I tried to play it cool when Finn walked through those doors, but everything in me screamed with aggravation. I had the instant urge to slap him. Mock him. Punch him. Kiss him. *Ugh.* I hated when the kiss part reared its ugly head.

Yes, I hated his guts, but he was hot as sin, and, yes, he got under my skin like no other man could, but there were parts of me that loved the back and forth bickering, picking fights, and winning them whenever he was around. I knew deep down he liked it too. Neither of us was ever going to act on it, though. Screw that. There wasn't enough patience in the world for me to give myself over to Finn Weston.

Finn was all reckless swagger, cocky comments, and pompous smirks, and he appeared to radiate an irritatingly dangerous air that I was drawn to, despite how much I wanted to hate him. He was gorgeous, with wavy dark brown hair, green eyes like emeralds, and the most chiseled jaw that seemed to be sculpted by the gods. If only he weren't the spawn of Satan.

All the guests were here, doors were closed now, and the engagement party had commenced. My eyes swung from Katie and Aaron, who were chatting with a few guests, to Finn, who was standing near the bar talking to a blonde. I had no idea who the blonde was, but she was most likely a co-worker or friend of Aaron's. I'd never seen her around my best friend, Katie.

"Are you okay?" Katie came to my side after I grabbed a drink from one of the bars.

"Yeah, of course. I'm great."

"Finn," she said, blinking at me, and that was the only name she needed to say to cause me a frown.

"What about him?" I couldn't meet her eyes, so I sipped my drink. Here I was again, unnerved beyond words by the presence of a man who despised me just as much as I did him.

Katie didn't fall for my cover-up. "Let's get out of here and talk about it. I know you and Finn are not the best of friends." She locked arms with me and lead the way through the room, ignoring my cries of protest.

"What about the guests?" I asked.

"Jessica can take over, " Katie insisted. Jessica was Katie's assistant. "That's what I hired her for."

When we were in the hallway, away from the music and chatter, Katie said, "I need to talk to you about Finn. You guys have to get along, or this will never work—for any of us."

"Impossible," I grumbled beneath my breath. "I can't stand him, Katie. Seriously. I'm trying to be cordial, but...ugh. There's just something about his stupid face that makes me want to slap it."

Katie laughed and shook her head. "Such strong urges, Rach."

"Well, it's true!" I sipped my drink.

I was never going to get along with Finn after the way he'd treated me. My first impression of him was horrible and, in my eyes, unforgivable. Here's what happened: Aaron and Katie had decided to host a party together. I'd arrived for the party before the couple, jetlagged from my long flight from New York, and spent the evening running errands for her that she'd asked me to do before retiring to the bed in my hotel suite, completely exhausted. But as I got comfortable and was starting to drift off to sleep, I was rudely awakened in the night by a noise from the next room.

I sat up in the bed groggily as the noise got louder, and then I heard words like:

"Oh, yeah."

"Oh, God."

"Damn, that's so good!"

"Mmmm...yeah, baby! Right there! Just like that...don't stop, don't stop!"

People were having sex next door, and not quietly, mind you.

I plopped back into the bed and threw a pillow over my head, but it seemed they only got louder, so I banged on the wall, hoping it would shut them up. That didn't help either. I kid you not, they became even louder.

I couldn't sleep for the rest of the night, even after the thumping stopped (and it didn't completely stop. The thumping resumed at least three more times, each when I tried dozing off), so I made some coffee and read over one of my client's portfolios to occupy myself instead.

It wasn't long before I heard voices in the hallway. I ran to the door and pressed my eye to the peephole, watching as they said their goodbyes. There was a man in an unbuttoned shirt, his hair dark and disheveled, a strong jawline, and a brunette with a short, tight red dress on.

I silently cursed the previous night's antics next door and badly wanted to open the door and embarrass them—ask them if they'd had a great time fucking the shit out of each other and not letting people sleep, but I didn't. And I was glad I didn't because when Aaron introduced Finn to me at the party, I was shocked to see he was the man in the suite next door to mine.

I had to tell Katie all about it, so I sent a text to her that said: **Aaron's shithead best friend was next door to me last night banging some girl like there was no tomorrow. You can thank him for the bags under my eyes. Men are such jackasses.**

But what I didn't realize in my haste to tell Katie was that I'd sent the text to the group chat I had going with Katie and Aaron, and while the party happened, Finn happened to be holding onto Aaron's phone, and he saw my text.

I had no idea Finn had seen it at the time, not

until he came up to me while I was at the bar, introduced himself, and then said, "I think you're just upset and a little jealous because no one was fucking *you* last night."

I was so shocked by his rude comment and so overcome with rage that I threw my champagne right at his face. Didn't think twice, just tossed it at him. Served him right for being such an arrogant jackass. He had no right to say that to me, whether it was a joke or not. Then again, I was the one who'd technically started it by calling him a shithead in the text, but he was never supposed to see said text, and if he were wise and mature enough, he would have ignored my text altogether and pretended it never happened. But he didn't. He decided to be an actual dickhead to me after reading it. I'd embarrassed him and he'd embarrassed me, and we were two embarrassed, angry people at a party who had silently declared our hate for each other at that very moment. And that's the story.

I looked from Katie and down the hallway, spotting Finn standing by the window with Aaron. He was looking right at me. I rolled my eyes as he narrowed his. For someone who hated me so much, he sure did stare a lot.

Katie looked over her shoulder at me and sighed. "Just ignore him, Rachel."

"Do you mean the fire-breathing dragon who looks like he wants to bite my head off? You want me to ignore *that*? Sure, Katie. It's not like I don't try to ignore him every time he shows his arrogant face, and it's not like he doesn't despise every fiber in my body."

She took my hand in hers and squeezed it. "Come on. He doesn't despise you. You're far too good for someone to dislike. You two just had a rocky start, but I'm sure it can get better if you at least try."

"It'll never get better. He's an ass. End of discussion."

"Ugh, Rach." Katie sighed.

"Don't worry. I'll be on my best behavior tonight and for the rest of your wedding events. I promise, Katie."

"Okay. I'm holding you to that promise. I told Aaron to talk to Finn too, so you both have made promises, and you have to keep them."

We walked slowly toward Finn and Aaron, and a discomfort settled in my belly. Finn fixed his eyes on me and I looked away, trying my hardest not to roll mine or make a disgusted face. While Aaron and

Katie spoke, I looked up to meet his gaze that held so many feelings.

Aggravation.

Disdain.

Desire.

I ignored the last part and forced a smile at him. For as long as I was to be around him, I would never cave. He fucked anything with legs, and I was sure he'd shove his hate for me aside to take a nip at me, but there was no way in hell I was giving myself to him. He was undeserving, and not only that, but none of us needed those lines blurred. Katie and Aaron were getting married, and they were our best friends. Even if Finn were to drop to his knees and beg my forgiveness or show even an ounce of humility, we could never be.

CHAPTER FOUR

RACHEL

Two Years Later

"I'm losing it." I groaned, staring up at the clock on the wall. It was nearing two in the afternoon. My hair was swinging down toward the carpet as I lay upside down on the sofa, bare heels up against the wall.

"Rach, what is going on with you?" Pam asked from the other end of the line. Pam was my sister, and I could hear typing, phones ringing, and people chatting in the background. She was at work, like always, and for the first time, I envied that. I needed a job. Stat.

"Oh, nothing. Just hoping all the blood will rush to my head and I can pass out, so I don't have to keep looking for jobs anymore."

"Well, I need you to perk up, Rach. Get on the laptop and keep submitting applications."

Pam still thought it was *that* easy. I couldn't blame her. It almost always was for her, but she was six years older than I was and had had more opportunities than I did. I'd been applying for jobs going on three months now, ever since losing my publicity job in New York. It was so sudden and, honestly, depressing. We got called into the conference room and were told the business was bankrupt and would be shutting down within two weeks. It was such short notice and after a month, I couldn't afford my expensive Manhattan studio anymore and that, on top of my credit card and student loan debt, caused me to come running right back to Los Angeles.

I was temporarily living in Katie's condo that she'd normally leased to tenants since she moved in with Aaron. She allowed me to stay there until I got another job and my own place to stay. Katie was a great friend. I swear sometimes I didn't deserve her.

Katie was now happily married and living with Aaron in a mansion in Malibu. She posted on Instagram daily, sharing pictures of herself by the pool or on a trip abroad, living her best life. I couldn't even say how much I dreamed of a life like hers.

I heaved a sigh, "Maybe I should just get married to some rich old guy. That would solve all of my problems."

"That doesn't sound very promising," Pam replied cheekily.

"I'd have all my debt cleared, a maid, and I could go shopping whenever I want. I'd have to satisfy a wrinkly penis here and there, but that's worth spending all his money, I guess."

Pam busted out laughing. "Ew, Rachel! I do *not* want to picture old, wrinkly penises!"

I laughed with her and then groaned again.

"Listen," Pam said, and I heard her stop typing. "Stop wishful thinking and make something happen. Right now is the best time to look for a job. College students are going back to school, which means more positions are opening. Have you tried any secretary or assistant jobs?"

"Ugh. I was a high-dollar go-to publicist, Pam. I can't be a secretary. *I* had a secretary!"

"Well, you have to start somewhere, hun. Los Angeles is stiff competition if you're trying to start your own company there. Look, I have to go, but I'll call you when I'm off. Love you."

"Love you too." I hung up the phone and tossed it to the opposite end of the sofa. I sat up swiftly, a dizzy spell hitting me as I felt the blood rush to the rest of my body, then I took a deep breath, glancing around the tiny apartment. Katie lived here once; now, she resided in a mansion with six bedrooms, a pool and sauna, and a view of the beach.

It was time to get out of the situation I was in and do better for myself.

I stood up and walked over to the kitchen table, which served as a desk for me as well. I turned on my laptop and waited for it to start up, then went to a job search website to search for secretary and assistant jobs.

I scrolled past some of the results, but the tenth one caught my eye. I clicked immediately.

Brewer Coffee Company: The perfect balance of cost and flavor...

I scrolled through the listing. They were looking for people who had a bachelor's degree, were accomplished, intelligent, problem-solvers, trustworthy, reliable, and able to pass a background check with no violations whatsoever.

The position?

Executive Assistant.

I read on.

We focus on an exclusive clientele.

Our client BCC needs an executive assistant to maintain and monitor the CEO's calendar of scheduled appointments, upcoming events, and matters requiring immediate attention.

Strict confidentiality is the first criteria, as well as promptness, due diligence, and openness for travel.

It sounded simple enough. At this rate, I had nothing to lose, so I uploaded my resume, filled out the application, and then went to find the next job that seemed promising.

CHAPTER FIVE

FINN

I was spending some time at Brotherhood Clubhouse, a place where rich men played cards, drank hard liquor, and smoked cigars. Often, business was debated, copious amounts of alcohol were consumed, and we spoke about rising companies to invest in to double or triple our money.

Jake Hunter was the one who told me about Brotherhood. We met once a week as a group of billionaires who used the night to escape their realities, marriages, and work.

I didn't particularly care for the Brotherhood, but I made myself participate because it presented endless opportunities and had boosted my career tenfold. Because of the Brotherhood, I was able to buy a coffee company that was about to go down in ashes several years ago. I rebuilt and rebranded it (which took me quite some time, and at one point, I thought it was going to fail under my orders too), and now it was one of the highest-grossing coffee companies to date...but that didn't come without a lot of borrowed money and sacrifices.

Jake had approached me five years ago when I was just getting started with the business, urging me to join the club and take advantage of its benefits. I'd finally agreed after a few drinks and a game of pool. Jake was only supposed to be helping me network at first, but he saw something in me and vouched for me to join Brotherhood.

Jake befriended me at a conference in Texas seven years ago, and we'd been really good friends ever since. I was strangely happy to have another friend I could hang out with since Aaron was living blissfully in Malibu with Katie. Aaron seemed to have less time to spend with me because he was always with her. It made sense, but it also made for lonely times. Jake came in handy when I felt loneliness sinking in.

“So, you’re on the hunt for another assistant, huh?” Jake asked.

We were seated at the bar, taking a break from poker.

“Yes. The former assistant was horrible. She double booked me and made me look like a complete ass in front of Wester. She had to go.”

“Damn, man.” Jake sipped his drink. “That sucks. You have to be careful with who you hire next.”

I took a sip of my scotch. “Yeah, I will this time. Audrey is doing the hiring process, but she knows to be meticulous about who to hire. She can’t have her job on the line too.”

"Wise choice. So,” he said, grinning, “making any progress with Ariel?"

My smile instantly disappeared at his question. I knew if I’d touched my forehead, I'd find deep lines gathered there. Ariel was my ex-girlfriend. She was also a social media influencer and the daughter of one of the billionaires who’d funded my company.

After our breakup—and because she’d cheated on me with some corny kid while she was in Paris—she requested that we kept up appearances to avoid scandalous stories about her. I didn’t so much care that she’d cheated. I wasn’t taking her seriously anyway, and we hardly spent time together, so it didn't bother me. When she asked me to keep up appearances, I agreed out of respect for her father. It was getting a little tiresome for me, though. Sometimes she didn't know the difference between *pretending* to be in a relationship and actually *being* in one. We were no longer an item, and as badly as I wanted to let her go completely, I knew it was too much of a risk for my company.

"Honestly, I think Ariel is the penance for my sins. Enduring her theatrics is the price I have to pay for the life I have now," I said.

"Trust me, we all have prices to pay. But at this point, man," Jake started, "you just have to play your cards right. You might not feel like it, but the reality is you're sort of indebted to her family. Her father is your biggest investor, and he continues to invest in your company, thinking you two are a happy couple. If he finds out you're not or that you don't want anything to do with her, it won't just be about business to him. He'll take it personally and cut you off."

"I know." I drew in a deep inhale before exhaling. As I did, my phone chimed. There was an email from Audrey with the subject line: **I think we found the perfect assistant.**

I opened her email to read over the forwarded

application, and my heart practically dropped when I read the applicant's name.

Rachel Quinn.

Wow. Luck be damned.

CHAPTER SIX

RACHEL

I'd been waiting to meet the boss for two hours, and it already told me that he was clearly a very busy man. An hour of that time had been spent with Audrey, who gave me a tour around the building so I could get familiar with my surroundings. The other hour was spent meeting people I would be working with closely—everyone except the boss, who everyone called Mr. Weston.

I hated the name Weston. It reminded me of Aaron's jackass friend, Finn. But the last time I saw Finn several years ago, he was a nobody and could never own a company like this one. Whomever this

CEO Mr. Weston was, I hoped he was at least pleasant.

I'd been nervous since boarding the Uber that morning, and the heavy metal music that pulsed from the driver's stereo didn't help. Going up the elevators of the huge Brewer building had my nerves shot too.

This was a big job, a multi-billion-dollar company for which I had been selected for. I couldn't fuck this up.

I was doing my best to bottle up my nerves while I sat on the chair in front of the CEO's office, waiting for Audrey to return. I heard her heels click and a door open before she rounded a corner and smiled at me.

"Mr. Weston is in the conference room and has a moment. Let's go meet him."

I followed her across polished marble floors and down an immaculate hallway with portraits of various skyscrapers and buildings on the wall.

The discomfort I felt tripled, and the anxiety swirled in me like a whirlpool. What if he hated me on sight? What if I butchered the job the first day and got fired? Seriously, I couldn't afford to be jobless again. I *needed* this.

Audrey's walk was brisk as she sauntered into a

different section of the building with rooms that looked even more elegant than the department we'd left. She stopped in front of a door that said **Main Conference Room** and twisted the gold doorknob, opening the door to reveal a room that appeared to be made up of windows. Outside the windows were other buildings and skyscrapers that made up Downtown Los Angeles.

"Good morning Mr. Weston," Audrey said as we walked inside.

"Morning, Audrey," a deep, familiar voice said back.

My heart dropped at the sound of the voice. *Wait.* I knew that voice—the depth and smoothness of it. I stepped around her and saw the man sitting at the head of the table.

And *oh my God.* I couldn't believe my eyes.

It was *Finn fucking Weston.*

CHAPTER SEVEN

RACHEL

I had to hold on to the edge of the table to avoid falling over. How could I not have known?

Weston!

The name Weston had blindsided me completely. Even though I knew it was his name, I never actively used it in reference to him. I knew I hated it, but he was just *Finn*, and there were a lot of Weston's in the world. And last I'd heard from Katie around the time of her wedding, Finn's company was pretty mediocre. Granted, I didn't know he owned a coffee company, but now it all made sense. He was the CEO.

Finn rolled out of his chair, his green eyes locking on mine. With a smug smile in my direction, he said, "Thank you, Audrey, I'll take it from here." I knew that smile. I could see the mischief swirling in his eyes. He wanted this to happen, and why wouldn't he? It was a golden opportunity to make my life a living hell. Get revenge for the champagne I'd tossed in his face.

Audrey walked out of the room and closed the door behind her, and a part of me longed to follow right after her.

"Rachel Quinn," Finn said when she was gone. "Who would have thought I'd see you in *my* building." He was staring at me, his eyes intense.

My gaze swept over the Armani-clad gentleman who had his brows cocked as if waiting for me to react or lash out.

"I had no idea you owned this company," I said.

He grinned. "Surprise?"

"Look, Finn," I said, raising my hands in the air. I didn't have time for games. "If you have me here just to toy with me, then I may as well leave right now. I need a serious job, and we both hate each other, so this will never work."

"I never said I hate you, Rachel. I may get annoyed by your presence, and perhaps there are moments when I wish I could return the favor of tossing cold champagne in your face, but I don't hate you."

My shoulders sagged, but not with relief. Something in my gut told me this was still a horrible, horrible position to be in. I focused on the table in front of me, waiting for what he had to say next.

"But to remain professional, I do believe I should offer you an apology. So, I'm sorry, Rachel."

Apprehension immediately rose in me. "You're sorry?"

"Yes. I apologize for what I said to you last time we met. It was extremely rude of me."

"Um...okay. I suppose I accept your apology."

"Great. Now, if you could provide the same courtesy."

"What?" I yelped.

"An apology," he said, smirking. "That way, we can start from square one."

Wow. What a bastard. I should've known he wasn't sincere about his apology. I wanted to hurl my purse at his face, but I controlled myself. I needed this job. Not forever, but at least for right now, until I found another Public Relations company that would hire me.

"Finn, let's get real. I'm not going to apologize, so

you can either fire me right now or take what you get. I have a great resume and I'm a hard worker. If you want to pass up the opportunity of having me, then fine. But I won't be coerced to apologize for something that happened years ago—especially to a guy who didn't even mean his apology in the first place."

I kept my gaze even with his, and he walked around the large oval table until he was standing right in front of me. "I guess that's fair." His eyes traveled up and down the length of me. "Fine. You can stay. But only because I'm not dealing with HR on this shit. And there's no promising I'll make this job easy for you, *assistant*."

"I don't mind a little hard work, *boss*."

He made his way to the door with a cocky smirk. "Great. I'll keep that in mind as we move forward. Find Audrey. She'll get you squared away."

I watched him leave the room, and I swear I heard him laugh before disappearing out of my sight.

CHAPTER EIGHT

FINN

What the hell was I thinking keeping that fire-breathing woman around? Rachel was too damn distracting. The way she chewed on the end of her pens or her thumbnail, or the way she drank from the straw of her cups—fucking distracting. All I could think about was how there were so many things I could do to her mouth—so many ways I could fuck it but, of course, I couldn't act on it. She worked for me, and not only that, but I didn't like crossing the lines of business and pleasure with my employees.

At work today, her second day in the office now, I tried my best not to think about her presence. The fact that I had Rachel Quinn as my assistant, waiting at my beck and call, made me feel powerful—and malevolent, too. I wanted to reign over her, rule her, make her do tricks and backflips for me, just for the hell of it. Hell, maybe I could've had her deliver coffee to me on her knees. I had full control of her in the office, and she knew it, no matter how much she pretended I didn't, and something told me she needed this job. She probably assumed I hadn't caught her flex when she threw her resume talk at me, but I knew that game very well. Making herself seem irreplaceable or top priority, a loss to a man running a company such as mine. Please. She was still so full of herself.

Despite that, I couldn't focus with her around, so I decided to call up Jake for a tennis match. Finding distraction on the court had been easier than in the office, where she was just a few steps away. But now that I was under the shower with my hands no longer working away tensions with my racket, my brain was back to working overtime.

This wasn't going to work. Soon, I was going to have to find another assistant because, surely, I was going to piss Rachel off one of these days, or she was going to piss me off.

"So, what are you going to do about this Rachel

Quinn situation?" Jake asked. We were out of the showers and back in the locker room. Jake moved swiftly around his locker, already buttoning his black silk shirt. I'd told him all about Rachel the night the application was sent over to me. He didn't think it was wise of me to hire her, said I was playing with fire, but I figured she was applying for a reason. She had to know she would be working for me if she wanted the position. I figured she wanted to call our little feud off, but when I saw the look on her face in the conference room the first day she arrived, it told me everything I needed to know. She had no idea I was her boss, and her disdain for me had likely quadrupled.

"Nothing," I answered gruffly.

"What do you mean *nothing*? You know you can't keep her there forever."

"She got selected for the position because she's a good candidate. Everyone agrees, and it'd make me look like a complete ass to let her go just because I don't like her. Plus, right now, I need the best candidate working for me to close on the Thomas Hotels deal."

"So?" Jake's voice was genuinely interested.

"So, I keep her at arm's length, focus on my work, and treat her as my assistant. That's it. The past is the past. My company is more important than my dislike for an assistant."

Jake smiled, one of his sheepish smiles that indicated wheels of mischief were turning in his head. "I think you guys are attracted to each other. You should just book a hotel, fuck her, and get all that hate out of your systems. It'll serve you right."

"Yeah fucking right," I retorted. "I don't fuck my employees. That's a strict rule of mine."

"But you *are* attracted to her?" Jake mused.

I ignored his question and got dressed. Yes, I was attracted to her, but there was no way in hell I was about to admit that shit out for the universe to hear.

CHAPTER NINE

RACHEL

I rubbed my temples after placing my pen down. It was eight o'clock on a Friday night, and Finn had purposely made me stay late to complete his scheduling for the next month.

I knew he was giving me extra work to spite me and to see if I'd crack and quit, and to make matters worse, he'd gone through Audrey to do it. He never asked me to do the work directly. It was always Audrey coming to me or sending me emails. Scheduling his personal appointments, gym days, lunch, and dinner meetings was a job for Audrey, not me, but Audrey had a kid, and he found it only right to make me stay late and do it so that Audrey wouldn't miss out on time with her son. How do I know this? Because Audrey told me they were his exact words.

I picked my head up and looked out of the window at the towering skyscrapers ahead. Things could've been worse. I could've been stuck in Katie's hand-me-down condo looking at the same four walls all day, but I wasn't. I was in the Brewer building with an LA city view and had the whole office to myself.

Speaking of, my phone buzzed, and Katie's name popped up on the screen. I answered and put her on speaker.

"Hey, Katie Kat!"

"Hi, Rachie Rach!" she squealed into the phone. "What are you doing?" I could hardly hear her over the noise in the background.

"Where are you?" I asked.

"Oh—I'm at one of Aaron's work parties. It's fucking boring, and I've been drinking all night. Finn was here, but he left early. Said he had work to do."

"Oh. Cool." It annoyed me when she brought Finn up in our recent conversations like he was suddenly the most important thing in my life. He wasn't. At all. Just because I worked for him, it didn't change how much he worked my nerves.

"What are you doing tomorrow morning? I was thinking we could get pedicures and some breakfast."

"Oh, man, I'd love that," I sighed, but then I remembered I had to work in the morning for a few hours. Finn had a short conference, and I had to be there. "But I can't in the morning. Finn has something I have to be here for."

"Well, what about the afternoon? Pedicures and then lunch?"

"Afternoon is better."

The elevator chimed, and I looked to my left. I saw a silhouette pass by and go in the direction of Finn's office. *What the hell? I thought I had the office to myself.* "Katie, let me call you back."

I hung up and pushed away from my desk, walking down the hallway to see who the person was. I figured it was the custodian, but it wasn't. Finn's office door was wide open, and he was standing inside the room, peering out of the window. He wore a blazer over a button-down black shirt, but it was undone at the collar. His dark hair was tousled, hanging over his forehead, and a hand was on his hip as if he were contemplating many things about life. The office was still dark. He hadn't turned any of the lights on. It was like he wanted the room this way—like he did this sort of thing all the time.

"Finn?" I called, and he immediately whirled around, his eyes wide.

"Fuck, Rachel! You scared the shit out of me!"

"I scared *you*? All I saw was a huge black silhouette walking through the office, and I got freaked out. I almost called security."

"Yeah, well, it's just me." He looked me over and frowned a little. "Why are you still here anyway?"

"Um, because you told me to finish your schedule for the month." Jerk.

"Ah. Right. Forgot about that." He took off his suit jacket and tossed it on top of his desk, causing some papers to fly off and land on the floor.

"I'll get that," I sighed. I was still on duty, after all.

"No—don't bother. Seriously." Finn faced me, his head shaking. "I'm tired of everything being so damn perfect. Sometimes a little chaos is better."

"Sometimes it is...but in this case..." I paused, chewing on my bottom lip.

"Jesus, don't do that," he groaned.

"Do what?"

"That thing with your teeth and your bottom lip. It drives me crazy, Quinn."

Finn shifted sideways, and it didn't take a genius to know he was a little intoxicated.

"Katie told me you were at a work party with Aaron."

"I was. It sucked, so I left."

"Yeah. Katie said it was boring."

"Boring feels too nice of a word."

I huffed a laugh. "Have you been drinking?"

"A little."

"I hope you didn't drive like that."

"I'd never risk lives. Besides, I didn't drink at the party. I drank at the bar a block away from here. Came here to sleep it off on my sofa, but you're here, so..."

"Yeah, I'm here. And I'm almost done with your scheduling, so I'll be out of your hair soon enough." I started to turn away, but then I heard footsteps behind me.

A warm hand caught my elbow, and Finn twisted me around to face him. "Do you really hate me?" he asked.

My lips parted as I looked up into his sparkling green eyes. The city lights reflected off his irises, making them all the more alluring.

"I never said I hated you, Finn."

"But you act like it. I see it in your eyes." He lowered his head, and his lips were so close.

"Only because you act the same way."

"Well, you definitely get on my nerves," he retorted.

"And you get on mine too, jackass."

He huffed a laugh.

I fought a smile. He lingered in front of me for a while, and I could smell the liquor on his breath. I felt the heat of his lips near mine, and I wanted to shove him away, just to show him that his charm couldn't work on me, but I also wanted to reel him closer, taste the liquor on his lips. I wanted him to kiss me just to see what it felt like to kiss such an arrogant person. I hadn't been kissed in so long.

After losing my job, I hibernated and mostly kept to myself. Now I was back in the ring, restoring my confidence, and I couldn't believe I was thinking it, but I was even willing to take on Finn Weston to satisfy my womanly needs as of right now. It had to be the late night. My work overload was getting to me.

It wasn't long before Finn released my arm and took a step away. As if coming to his senses, he raked his fingers through his hair and said, "You should get back to work, Quinn. I'll see you tomorrow."

CHAPTER TEN

FINN

When I woke up the next morning, my head was pounding. After I'd practically pushed Rachel away, I found a half-empty bottle of whiskey in my desk drawer and finished it off, just to get rid of any illicit ideas I had of her.

But the illicit ideas didn't stay away for long. When I saw her leave, I took off my pants, crashed on the couch in my office, and fisted and pumped my cock until I came. Cum, dribbled over my fist when I released, some getting on my pants.

I imagined Rachel coming back into my office, forgetting my orders, and climbing on top of me to ride my cock. I imagined her getting off to suck my cum into her pretty little mouth and swallowing it all down.

It was wishful thinking, and I knew it, but damn, would it have been magnificent.

It was a new day now, and as I'd told Jake, I didn't fuck my employees. I disregarded all thoughts of Rachel as best as I could, grabbed the spare suit hanging in my office closet, and freshened up in my suite-style bathroom.

By the time 9 a.m. rolled around, and I'd swished my mouth with mouthwash, it didn't even appear as if I was hung over. I left my office to get to the conference room and heard the elevator. I noticed Rachel walking in with Audrey, and I hurried to the conference room before she could see me. I knew what I'd done last night was unprofessional. I touched her, came close to kissing her. I couldn't have her thinking that was the norm for me.

At the end of the day, my business came first, and I couldn't let it sink over drunk, late-night urges, and lust.

I sat at the head of the table, spreading my papers out. Audrey walked into the room, placed fresh pastries on the serving table, and then booted up the coffee maker. She told me good morning, I returned the greeting, and then she was out of the conference room to tend to her secretary duties.

My client had arrived, and Rachel escorted him in. She helped me organize my notes, and every time our eyes connected, I felt my cock ache.

Fuck. What was wrong with me? All of a sudden, I didn't hate Rachel and instead wanted to fuck her every which way. I blamed Jake for that—for putting the idea of fucking her until she was out of my system into my head. It didn't sound like such a bad idea anymore.

When the meeting was over, I knew I'd won Thomas Hotels over. Audrey and Rachel cleared the room and took the leftover pastries and coffee to the breakroom, and when Audrey left to attend her son's soccer game, Rachel sat at her desk to do more work.

I sat in my office, watching her for a moment. When her eyes would venture over to mine, I'd look away. Eventually, she'd finished up her tasks for the day and started packing, but it didn't feel quite right just to let her walk out of there. After last night, something had come over me. I wanted her close, even if we couldn't do anything together. But what the hell was I supposed to do about it?

"I'm meeting Katie for a pedicure. Is there

anything else you need from me before I go?" she asked when she met up to my door.

"No. I'm good, Quinn. Enjoy the rest of your day and tell Katie I said hello."

She nodded, her blonde curls swimming around her face. "Okay." She shifted on her feet, hesitant.

"Is there anything else?"

"It's...about last night," she started.

I did my best to remain neutral. "What about it?"

"It was true what I said. I don't hate you, Finn. And I think it would be nice if we can start being more mature about where we stand from now on. Plus, it would save our friends a lot of grief." She huffed a laugh.

I laughed too. "Yes. It absolutely would."

"So, what do you say?" she asked. "Can we start over?"

"Sure, Quinn. We can start over." I pushed out of my chair. "But only if you agree to get a drink with me tonight. You know, to celebrate our newfound friendship." I was a fool. Such a fucking fool. To me, drinks with a woman always meant sex. But with Rachel, it was different. I did want to start anew, give ourselves a fun night of drinking and a refresher. Yeah, that's what I told myself anyway.

"Um...okay. Sure. Just let me know what time and where."

"I'll text you."

"Okay." She gave me a smile and then turned away, making her way toward the elevator. As she went, I watched her round hips swing in her brown leather skirt.

And when she boarded the elevator, I realized I was way in over my head. I wanted to fuck Rachel Quinn like there was no tomorrow, and I wanted it to happen as soon as possible.

CHAPTER ELEVEN

RACHEL

Finn: Meet me at the bar at Skye Hotel. 9 pm.

Oh, shit. A hotel? I knew what that meant. Drinks at a hotel bar always lead to other things. The rooms at most hotels were only a short elevator ride away, and before you knew it, you were fucking until the alcohol was sweating out of your pores.

"Who are you texting over there?" Katie asked, and I immediately shut the screen of my phone off.

"Nobody. Just work stuff."

Katie sat across from me at our favorite vegan restaurant, holding her hand out and studying her cuticles. "This manicure is great. I almost don't want to use my fingers to eat."

I laughed, and Katie started talking about a trip she and Aaron had coming up in Hawaii. As she did, my mind wandered to the hotel thing with Finn. I had to keep things professional, but after last night, I felt the lines had blurred. Finn was so close to kissing me, and I *wanted* him to kiss me. I wanted him to drop me down on his desk and devour me whole, but when I woke up this morning, I came to my senses.

Finn was my boss, and sleeping with him could have posed so many workplace complications. And right now, I needed the checks. I was planning on moving out of Katie's condo soon and into my own, and I couldn't afford to lose what I was getting as his assistant. He paid me well—so well I didn't even want to bother searching for another job with a publicist just yet. Sure, I had to tolerate him, but we'd made peace today and had agreed to start fresh. The only issue now was sharing drinks at a hotel.

I couldn't say I didn't want to join him. I wanted Finn so damn bad, despite how often I felt the urge to slap some sense into him sometimes. And all I kept thinking was maybe all of our fighting and arguing and bickering had amounted to this: a hotel room to ourselves, fucking the shit out of each other until we'd had enough.

Hell, we were both professionals. Finn put work first, and so did I. Who was to say we couldn't sleep with one another *and* work together? People did it all the time. My happy-go-lucky bachelor uncle slept with his secretary, and they never crossed any lines. To this day, she still works for him and continues to separate their business from pleasure.

I could do that, too...the only downfall was I'd be handing over even more control to an already dominant and controlling Finn Weston.

"So, how is working with Finn anyway?" Katie asked, taking a sip of her tea.

"It's...okay." I studied my freshly painted nails. They were lime green. Katie said we were only getting pedicures, but since she'd offered to pay for both our nails, we got the full set together.

"Just okay?" she asked.

"Yeah. I mean, he's Finn. He can be an ass when he wants to be, but he's been pretty decent since hiring me."

"Wow. Sounds to me like you guys will be making up soon," she said, smiling wide and winking.

"Well, that's completely up to him. If he's nice, I'm nice. Simple." I forced a smile and wanted to tell her I was meeting him tonight for drinks, but I also didn't want to jump the gun. For all I knew, I could have had the wrong impression of what'd happened last night and about meeting for drinks, and he was really just trying to be friends. I didn't want to look like a dumbass to Katie by thinking he wanted more.

Being friends with him was fine...but something in my gut told me I was going to be in for so much more with him by the end of the night.

After lunch with Katie, I still had three hours before meeting Finn. I decided to go shopping for something nice to wear...not for him, of course, but for me.

I stopped at one of my favorite boutiques in town and found a one-shoulder black dress, grabbed a pair of heels, checked out, and then made my way home to shower, blow-dry and style my hair, and get dressed.

I couldn't help looking in the mirror before I left, thinking to myself that maybe I'd tried a little *too* hard for tonight. My legs were out –and freshly shaved, might I add–and my hair was curled to perfection thanks to my handy dandy curling iron. I looked hot in my dress. *Too* hot.

I sighed and went for my purse and keys. It was too late to try and change. I had to rock this outfit and make it seem casual for tonight, so I left the apartment and went to my car, curious how the night ahead with Finn would go.

CHAPTER TWELVE

FINN

I checked my watch for the time. It was five minutes 'til and Rachel hadn't arrived yet. I wouldn't have been surprised if she didn't show up. It wasn't like Rachel Quinn to appease me other than on the job, and she could have called a truce earlier for work purposes.

I flagged down the bartender and ordered another scotch. When he handed it to me, I sipped it slowly, peering up at the football game on the TV. I wasn't a huge organized sports person, but Aaron and Jake were. They often had Superbowl and March Madness parties, and I always attended for the food and booze and their company. Times like this made me miss scheduling things with Aaron just for the hell of it.

Before he was married, he had way more freedom, but with Katie gripping him by the balls, he had to ask for her permission to do everything. That was why I never wanted to get married. What was the point of restricting myself to one woman for the rest of my life and giving up ample freedom when I could have had any woman I wanted without all the stress?

"Let me guess. Scotch?" someone asked, and I turned my head, coming face to face with Rachel beside me.

And *fuck me*. She looked incredible. Her black dress was short, revealing long silky legs. Her hair was in luscious curls, and she'd even put on makeup. She wore makeup to work, but it was never like this. She'd put forth an effort, and I immediately straightened on the bar stool when I realized she wasn't just here for courtesy. She wanted something...and I sensed that something—or *someone*, rather—was me.

"It is scotch," I said. "How'd you know?"

"You always order scotch at parties," she said, taking the seat beside me. "And not only that, but you have a whole collection on a wall in one of the conference rooms." She smiled at me through her red-stained lips, revealing bright white teeth.

"Honestly, the bottles in the office are just for show," I said, smirking. "Do you want one?" I asked, lifting my glass.

"I'll take gin." She lifted a hand and flagged the bartender down herself. When she placed her order, she turned to look at me and said, "So I think we should create some kind of official agreement for what we talked about earlier."

I sipped and then said, "You mean like a written truce?"

"Yeah. Something like that. We agree to get along from now on, and if we don't, then I leave Brewer Coffee."

"Okay." I straightened myself on the stool again and extended an arm, offering a hand to her. "We can agree to get along from now, and if one of us has an issue, then we'll part ways and pretend the other doesn't exist."

"Exactly." She grabbed my hand and shook it. I closed my hand around hers and smiled. "Let the truce commence."

CHAPTER THIRTEEN

RACHEL

"So, who was the girl you had at that hotel that night anyway?" I asked. I was referring to the night that initially sparked my aggravations toward Finn.

"Oh. Her name was Ariel."

"Ah. Ariel. Does she sing like The Little Mermaid to you often?" I mused.

Finn laughed at my cheesy joke and shook his head, nursing his second scotch since I'd arrived. "Not often. Trust me. And what about you? I've never seen you with a guy. What's up with that?"

"Yeah, well, that's because I don't exactly believe in relationships. The last one I had was in college and lasted all four years. The night we graduated, I found him in a room with a cheerleader, so..." I shrugged and hoped he could tell the memory didn't still pain me. I don't think I passed the nonchalance, though, because there was a small ounce of sympathy written all over his face and buried deep in his glazed green eyes.

"Well, if you're ever to call anyone a jackass again, it should be him," said Finn.

"Right. Yeah. But I don't plan on *ever* seeing him again, so I guess I'll have to keep using it on you." I winked and grinned before sipping my second gin.

"If it makes you feel better, The Little Mermaid cheated on me too."

"Oh my gosh! Seriously?"

"Yeah. But I didn't care," he said, shrugging. "I wasn't really taking her seriously."

"So why did you bother dating her then?"

Finn shrugged again and sighed. Then he changed the subject by asking, "Do you really think I'm a jackass? I mean—okay, yes, I know I can be a little uptight and controlling, but a *jackass*?"

"Finn, Aaron told me you hate riding in the car with other people because you *have* to drive. You literally can't hand over control with a task as simple and ordinary as *driving*. And don't even get me started on the office control. If a person is even a minute late, you're flipping out about it like a maniac." I winced. "Don't fire me because I said that, though. That's just the liquor talking."

"I would never fire you," he said, smiling a little.

"Never ever?"

"No. You're incredible at the office, and everyone likes you. Audrey thanks me every time you take a load off for her."

"Aww, Finn! That's the nicest thing you've ever said to me! Literally!"

"Come on now, don't get mushy on me." He sipped again. "But I will say, it's nice to be out right now. I don't really get to hang out and just chill and drink without thinking about work much anymore. I used to with Aaron, but he's so busy with Katie these days that it's hard to catch much of any time with him."

"Oh, trust me. I get that. Me and Katie were like peas in a pod at one point in our lives. Now we've sort of created new lives away from each other, and it's a little sad to think about how little time we spend together now."

"Yeah. We're getting older," Finn said. "And Aaron is happy, and he deserves it, so I don't complain. But sometimes, I do miss jumping at opportunities with him."

"Well, hey, we can jump at all the opportunities together from now, since we've formed our truce and all."

"That's true." He lifted his glass in the air. "Cheers to that, Quinn."

I tapped my glass to his "Cheers."

CHAPTER FOURTEEN

FINN

It was nearing two in the morning, and I couldn't get enough of Rachel. I had planned on cutting it short to an hour max with her if I got even the slightest bit annoyed, but our conversations were effortless. I felt myself unloosening, unwinding, and getting comfortable with her. I didn't realize she and I had so much in common and felt like we should have called this truce sooner.

We were both feeling our drinks, and sweat was beading at my brow line from drinking so many scotches. I loosened my tie and adjusted on the stool, and Rachel checked the time on her phone.

"It's getting late," she murmured.

"Yeah. It is. And I have a brunch in the morning. No mimosas for me. I can already feel a hangover brewing."

"Well, I should get going then." Rachel polished off her drink and then collected her purse and phone from the counter. When she stood up, I followed suit.

"Let me walk you out," I offered, and she nodded.

I walked with her through the bar of the hotel and to the lobby. When we were out the door, I asked, "Did you drive?"

"Yes. One of Katie's cars."

"Are you okay to drive?" I asked, and as soon as I did, she stumbled a bit.

"Um..." she sputtered a laugh.

"Damn, Rachel. I don't think I should let you drive. Remember the engagement party when you took my keys?" I stuck my hand out. "Well, I'm gonna need yours now."

"No way!"

"Yes, way. Your keys, Quinn. I'll book you a room here, and you can sleep it off until you're sober. I'm not letting you drive like this."

She looked at me reluctantly and then at the

street where a few cars were driving by. "Okay, fine. But we're not sharing a room, are we?"

"Of course not," I laughed. I hooked my arm through her elbow. "Come on."

We went back into the hotel, and I requested two rooms at the counter.

"I'm sorry, sir, but we only have one more room for the night, and it's a penthouse King suite," the receptionist said with an uneasy smile. "There was a wedding this weekend, so we're low on accommodations."

"Are you serious right now? There's nothing at all?" Rachel pleaded.

"I'm afraid not," the receptionist said anxiously.

"There are hotels nearby," I offered Rachel. "We could walk to one." She pressed her lips and shook her head. "Are you kidding? There's no way I can walk in these heels. Screw it. We'll share until I'm sobered up, but you have to take the couch, bud."

"Fine by me."

I booked the room, collected the key card, and went to the elevator with Rachel. She stood in the corner opposite of me inside the elevator and gave me a lazy smile. I smiled back and shook my head. "What's so funny?"

"You," she snickered. "Pretending you aren't

excited to share a room with your worst enemy. I bet you can't wait to brag about this to your homies."

"Okay, first of all, don't ever use the word homies again. What are we, in fifth grade?"

She busted out laughing.

"Second of all, there's no reason for me to tell them about this. We're simply sharing a room for a few hours because we're both too drunk to drive."

"Mm-hmm," she said in a sing-song tune.

The elevator doors peeled open, and I walked out first, leading the way to the room. Shoving the key card in the slot, I twisted the handle and walked into the immaculate suite that provided a city view of downtown Los Angeles.

Rachel came in after me, in awe of the view too. The room became completely dark when the door shut behind her, and she stood next to me, staring ahead at the velvety midnight blue sky and the lights twinkling on the skyscrapers. A plane was flying in the distance and appeared to have just taken off.

"It must be nice to pay for places like this and get views like these without any financial worries," Rachel said breathily.

"It is nice...but it sucks sometimes when there's no one to share the views with."

"Well, we're sharing this moment right now, aren't we?"

I turned a fraction to face her. "We are, huh?"

Her blue eyes swooped up to mine, and she smiled. "You're actually a really decent human being, Finn."

"And you're not as self-righteous as I thought, Quinn."

She giggled. "Our names rhyme."

Damn it. I couldn't stand this anymore. Beneath the milky light of the moon, she was even more beautiful, and perhaps I was drunk and stupid, but one thing was for certain—I wanted to kiss her.

With that in mind, I turned her toward me, cupped her face in my hands, and planted my lips on hers, taking what I'd been aching for since last night.

CHAPTER FIFTEEN

RACHEL

I couldn't wrap my mind around what was happening fast enough, but I quickly came to the realization that Finn had his lips on mine and was groaning like he'd wanted this to happen for a very long time.

And who was I to pretend I hadn't wanted the same thing too? I threw my arms around the back of his neck, and he groaned again, picking me up in his strong arms and carrying me toward the king-sized bed.

When he laid me on my back, he pushed between

my legs, and his mouth came down to my throat. He kissed me ravenously, and I wrapped my legs around his waist and brought my hands to his face, forcing his lips back on mine. They felt too good to lose.

"Rachel," he said. His voice was breathy and guttural. "Should I stop?" he asked.

"No. Don't." I held him closer, locking my legs around him.

He looked down at me with soft green eyes, then dove back down to kiss me passionately. I threaded my fingers through his hair, and when he pressed his erection between my thighs, I instantly wondered what he'd feel like inside me.

I broke the kiss and forced him to lean up so I could unbuckle his belt. He watched me lower his pants while on his knees on the bed, and when his boxers were down too, he held my chin between his thumb and forefinger and said, "I've been dreaming about your mouth, Quinn."

"Yeah?"

"Yes. And all the things I wanna do to it."

"What do you wanna do to it?" I asked.

"I want to *fuck* it," he said in a near growl. "I want to see what you look like with those pretty pink lips wrapped around me."

"Then do it," I challenged. "Fuck my mouth, Finn."

"Say no more." He gripped the base of his cock and brought the tip of it to my lips. I spread my lips apart, and he entered my mouth slowly. His mouth gaped as I closed my lips around his thickness, and then he sighed and held the back of my head, guiding himself deeper down my throat. "Shit, that feels so good," he groaned. He went deeper until he was touching the back of my throat. "If only we still hated each other, then I could hate fuck your mouth right now."

He pulled away, and when he did, I gasped and said, "Let's pretend we still do. I'm sure it won't be too hard."

He smiled down at me, then clutched a handful of my hair, bringing his cock back to my mouth and shoving it between my lips. I moaned around him, and he stared down at me with an intense gaze that made my body roll with pleasure.

"How does it feel having the man you hate's cock in your mouth?"

I moaned.

"You've wanted this since the first night we met, haven't you?"

I sighed around him. Yes, I wanted it, despite

how much I couldn't stand him. He was so devilishly handsome, and I wanted him in every way.

"Fuck, you look so good with me in your mouth," he rasped. "So sexy."

He pulled out of my mouth, and I sucked in a breath. Then he went straight for my dress, lifting it up and taking it off me. He noticed my matching red lingerie and smiled like he'd just discovered gold. "Seems I wasn't the only one who wanted this to happen, was I? I know the saying about women and their matching lingerie."

I smiled up at him and said, "Oh, shut up and fuck me already." Then I clasped his face in my hands and brought his body down on mine.

CHAPTER SIXTEEN

FINN

I was on top of her, but there was a problem. "I left my condoms in my car," I said quickly.

She kept kissing me. "Don't worry. I'm protected."

Relief hit me, and I went back to matching her kisses while taking off her panties. When she was completely bare, I sat up and took off my shirt, peeling out of it and then bending down to eat her out.

She shrilled with pleasure as I swirled my tongue around her clit over and over again until she came, then I pushed up on my knees, wasting no time gripping my cock and entering her slowly.

She gasped when she felt me, and our eyes locked. And the deeper I went, the more her mouth gaped and the harder it was for me to control the primal groan building up in the caverns of my chest.

So filled with pleasure, I kissed her soft and fucked her hard, and she moaned and kissed me back. One arm craned around the back of my neck as she took every one of my deep strokes.

I dropped my head and saw where our bodies were connected. She was sopping wet, drenching my cock.

"You really wanted me, huh?" I murmured.

"I did," she said back.

"You're so wet, and you look so good with me inside you." She clenched around me and leaned up to kiss me again. Her tongue curled around mine, and that was my trigger.

I plunged my tongue between her lips, groaning as I came inside her.

She gasped as I throbbed and released, and *shit*, I'd never felt so good. It was magical coming inside this woman—a woman I formerly couldn't stand. Now she was below me, taking every ounce of my cum, and it made me feel like the most powerful man in the world.

"Shit, Rachel," I panted. "That was...." *Incredible. Mind-blowing.* I wanted more. So much more.

"Wow, Finn," she panted. "I didn't know you had that in you," she teased as I pulled out.

"You'd be surprised what all I have in me." I flopped down beside her, and we both stared up at the ceiling, catching our breaths.

"Just so we're clear," she started, her hand coming down to my semi-hard cock. "No one can know about this." She began to stroke me, and it felt so good. "*No one,* Finn. Especially not Katie and Aaron." She gripped me in her palm, then ran a thumb over the head of my cock.

"Okay," I breathed. It was all I could do. I was getting hard again from her touch, but then she climbed on top of me, just like my fantasy the night before, and my cock became as stiff as a board.

"Promise," she said softly, leaning down to kiss me.

"I promise." She was grinding on my cock, then she sat up, lifted her hips, gripped me so that I was at a proper angle, and sank down on it, making my cock disappear inside her.

"Oh, fuck," I growled. "Fuck, Rachel. I'm gonna come again."

"You swear you won't tell?" she breathed, slowly riding my cock. She shifted her hips forward and backward, and I could feel myself about to explode.

"You have my word. No one...no one will know."

A smile swept across her lips, and then she picked up her pace, bouncing up and down on me, grinding forward and backward, and then winding her hips in full circles until I was left with no choice but to throw my head back, clutch her hips, and come again.

"Ah, Rachel!" I moaned, my cum pumping into her all over again. Some of it dripped out as she slowly lifted up and down my length and purposely made a mess with it. I met her eyes, and from the confidence buried within them, it was like she was trying to tell me without saying who the real boss was.

"Good," she murmured, leaning forward and kissing my lips. "You swore. And for once in your life, you gave up control." She smiled smugly, kissing me again, and I couldn't help but laugh. "There will officially be more of where that came from as long as this stays between us for now."

She climbed off and laid beside me.

And all I could think was *wow*. I was really enjoying this naughty, sexy side of Rachel Quinn.

CHAPTER SEVENTEEN

RACHEL

When I woke up the next morning, I felt a warm body spooning me from behind, and I had a hard time fighting my smile as I remembered exactly where I was. Finn was still with me, cuddling me, and I refused to move and ruin this moment.

I rested my head on my pillow again and felt him shift. Something hard dug into my back, and then he groaned.

"Looks like someone didn't get enough," I murmured.

"Not nearly enough," he said in a gruff, sexy

morning voice. His mouth came to my earlobe to say, "You think six times is too many?"

"Nope," I murmured, and he chuckled while lifting my leg, positioning himself behind me, and thrusting in deep. I gasped, looking at the floor-to-ceiling window ahead of me. The sun was rising in the California sky, and Finn Weston was fucking me slowly while moaning in my ear.

"I can't get enough of you, Quinn."

I couldn't get enough of him either, and that said a lot about him. It was hard for men to hook me. After college, I made it my mission to focus on my own life more than dating, but this thing I was doing with Finn was fun and promiscuous, and though he was technically my boss, it didn't feel wrong.

"Shit, Rachel." He let out a guttural groan as he stilled behind me, and I felt his cock pulsing as he came. He brushed my hair away from my ear and said, "You're so damn good."

"And you're not too bad yourself, boss."

Pulling away, he rolled to the other side of the bed and stood up. I turned over, bringing the sheet up to my chest.

"Excuse me. Are you trying to be modest?" he asked, smirking.

"Feels different now that there's the whole daylight and sobriety thing and all," I joked.

He laughed. "Right. I'm gonna hit the shower."

"Okay."

I watched him walk to the bathroom before throwing my head back on the pillow and staring up at the ceiling fan with a grin.

A phone vibrated, and my gaze fell to the nightstand. It was Finn's phone. When I heard the shower start up, I rolled over to check the screen. There was a message from Ariel.

Babe, please don't be late for brunch.

Dad will be pissed if you are.

I frowned.

Babe? Why was he having brunch with her dad? Was he seriously about to leave here after a night with me to be smitten with her? *Oh, hell no!*

I slid back to my side of the bed, my smile completely vanished. Ariel. She was the girl he was sleeping with in the hotel room next door to mine before we first met. The girl who apparently cheated on him, yet he still stayed in touch with her? Who was to say he hadn't lied about that? Or that he wasn't still having sex with her?

God, I was so stupid. So, so stupid.

I sat up and shoved the sheet away to collect my clothes. I knew I had no right to be upset. We were only having sex, that's all, but I couldn't help feeling a little...used.

I cleaned myself up as best as I could without using the bathroom and got dressed, still with the scent of him on me. When I heard the shower shut off, I found my purse on the floor, snatched it up, and walked out of the hotel room, making my way toward the elevator and refusing to look back.

CHAPTER EIGHTEEN

FINN

"What do you say we order room service?" I called from the bathroom. I wiped the condensation from the mirror and ran my fingers through my damp hair.

There wasn't an immediate response, so I walked out. "Quinn—" I clamped my mouth shout when I saw the room was empty. "Rachel?"

A frown overcame me as I looked around the suite. *Where the hell did she go?* I figured maybe she'd left a text to let me know where she'd run off to, so I picked up my phone, but there was only a text from Ariel.

. . .

Babe, please don't be late for brunch.

Dad will be pissed if you are.

I let out an irritated sigh. I couldn't stand when she called me babe, knowing we weren't actually together. She was so delusional about us.

Wait. Was this why Rachel ran off? Had she seen this message?

Oh shit.

What the hell had I done?

CHAPTER NINETEEN

RACHEL

Everything was fine. It was Monday morning, a new day, and the weekend was behind me. I'd had my fun with Finn, but now it was back to business. The pleasure side of things was over, we'd made our truce, and now we could go back to being professionals.

Those were the words constantly running through my mind as I made my way to work, but I couldn't stop thinking about Finn, and it annoyed the hell out of me because this guy was clearly dating someone.

There was no way I could continue sleeping with him, even if we did keep it secret. And the fact that he was meeting her and her dad proved that they were probably very serious.

I didn't know what he had going on with her, but I imagined him getting engaged or married to this Ariel girl. There was no way I was going to become a mistress. No fucking way. He was great in bed, but I had morals and standards, and being anyone's mistress was far beneath me.

I pulled into the parking deck of the Brewer building, and when I parked, I collected my things from the passenger seat. I drew in several breaths as I entered the private elevator that took me to the top floor, and when the doors parted ways, I spotted Audrey sitting at her desk.

She waved at me and said, "Morning! I got you some coffee. It's on your desk. Figured you'd need it for the long day ahead."

"Thanks Audrey." I forced a smile at her and was grateful she went back to typing on her computer. I wasn't up for much chit-chat.

I placed my handbag down on my desk and picked up the coffee cup that had my name and a smiley face on it. I smiled at the smiley face, wishing I was as chipper as Audrey was, but I wasn't. Finn would be coming into the office in about five minutes, and I wasn't sure how I was going to pretend we didn't fuck like animals the past weekend, or worse, pretend I didn't walk out on him.

I could've lied and told him I had something come up, but deep in my gut, I knew he wasn't going to believe me.

I sat and booted up my computer, and while it launched to the home screen, I opened my planners and notebooks and organized the pens in my cup.

The elevator chimed, and I braced myself as the doors parted. Out he walked, dressed in a tailored navy-blue suit with a sky-blue tie. His hair was gelled back, and he'd shaved since the night at the hotel. He looked...refreshed. Probably because he'd had a great brunch with his lover and her dad. I rolled my eyes at the thought.

"Morning, Audrey," Finn said as he passed her desk.

"Morning, Mr. Weston. Can I get you some coffee?"

"Yes, please. But have Rachel bring it in, will you?" he asked, and then his eyes flickered to mine. "Rachel, there are some things I want to discuss with you." I pressed my lips. I should've known he'd bring that control and demand right back into the office.

Audrey looked back at me as he walked into his office, and I nodded to let her know I'd heard him. I went to the breakroom and poured his coffee in a mug, placed it on a tray, and then added sugar and cream to the tray as well. He liked to pour it in himself.

I carried it past Audrey and into his office, where he was standing in front of his desk, peeling himself out of his suit jacket while reading over a paper placed on the edge of his desk. Most likely his schedule for the day that Audrey printed and left there.

I cleared my throat at the door, and his eyes lifted.

"Where would you like to have your coffee today, sir?" I asked, doing my best to keep the sass out of my voice.

"By the sofa."

I carried it to the coffee table in front of the leather sofa that faced the window. After placing it down, I was about to make my way back to the door and my desk, but he said, "Close the door a moment. I'd like to speak with you privately."

I glanced at him, and he raised his chin and cocked a brow, giving me a look that screamed, *"You aren't going anywhere until you explain yourself."*

I closed the door and faced him, my chin held high. "What is it you'd like to talk about, *sir*?"

"Oh, for Christ's sake, Rachel. Don't give me that *sir* shit right now. You know exactly what this is about."

I pursed my lips. "I don't think it's wise to talk about it in the workplace."

"Okay. Fine. But just tell me why you left."

"I had something come up." I avoided his eyes.

"You saw Ariel's message, didn't you?" he asked, taking a step toward me.

"I don't know what you're talking about."

"Yes, you do. You know exactly what I'm talking about. Rachel, Ariel and I aren't really together. You have nothing to worry about when it comes to her."

"Are you sure? Because meeting a woman and her dad for brunch seems pretty serious to me, Finn." I shrugged. "Just saying."

He sighed and walked closer to me. "Look, her father invests in my company. I keep up appearances with her, so he'll continue to invest. She agreed to us doing it. It was her idea."

"That's stupid," I muttered when he was only a step away from me.

"No. What's stupid is you running out of the room before giving me the chance to explain."

"What does it matter? We're only *doing* it. Nothing more, right?"

"You can't deny that we had a great time that night, Quinn."

I kept my mouth shut. No, I couldn't deny it, but I wasn't about to admit it to him.

Finn looked me over, studied my face. "This Thursday I'll be flying to Las Vegas," he said. "Viking Hotels is looking for a coffee distributor, and Audrey won't be able to make it because she has to tend to her son, so I'll need you there. It's an important pitch, and you're organized about these things."

"What if I can't make it?"

"Dropping everything to travel as my assistant is in the job requirements," he said, looking down at me. "You'll come, we'll share another hotel room, and we'll have a great time again." He'd backed me up against the door, his body pressing to mine and his lips only a sliver away. The heat of his body brought warmth to my cheeks and made me weak in the knees. All I could remember was the way he'd made me his on Saturday night and how we kept going back for more, over and over again.

I wanted to do that again...but I wasn't going to confess it outright. He was already arrogant enough.

"Fine," I stated.

He put on one of his smug smiles. "You're so

lucky I'm at work, or I'd kiss you right here, right now."

Heat unfurled in my belly, but I pretended to be unbothered by his statement. "I have to get back to work."

He nodded and continued to smile, stepping away and giving me space to move away from the door. I glanced back at him before walking out, letting my hair curtain my face so Audrey couldn't see how flustered I was. I was blushing ridiculously hard, and when I sat at my desk, I picked up my coffee while cracking a smile.

I swear, there were times when I couldn't stand him. But the times when I could tolerate him...God, he drove my mind and body crazy.

CHAPTER TWENTY

FINN

I flipped my wrist and checked the time. "Come on, Rachel. Where the hell are you?"

I stood on the stairs of the private jet and scoped the landing strip. I'd told her to be there on time, but of course, she was late. She probably thought I'd take off without her, which would leave her no choice but to stay in California.

A car drove toward the fence, and I saw a woman get out of the backseat. Blonde hair twisted in the wind. It was her. The driver helped her take out a suitcase, and then she walked through the gate after showing the security guard her badge.

"It's about damn time!" I shouted when she was within earshot.

"I'm sorry! I had to catch a ride!"

I walked down the steps and grabbed her suitcase. "Why didn't you just ask me? I could've picked you up."

She scoffed. "Yeah, no thanks on that. I'm good."

I shook my head and laughed, going back up the stairs with the handle of her suitcase in hand. Over my shoulder, I said, "When are you going to learn to lower your guard and actually trust people?"

"I do trust people," she said, following after me. "I just don't trust *you*." Her smile was smug, and I chuckled, stepping inside the plane.

"Wow." Rachel whistled as she stepped into the air-conditioned jet. "Fancy, Weston. Who are you trying to impress? I hope it isn't me."

"Please. This isn't my first time using a jet." I placed her bag in one of the compartments above.

She took one of the window seats and sighed. The leather, I was sure, was cool and comfortable, and I could tell she was enjoying it. The stewardess told me the pilot was preparing for takeoff, so I sat in the seat across from her and buckled in. She followed suit.

As the plane lifted, I looked into her eyes, and

she stared right back. "Why would you drag me on this trip? You know you can close on Viking Hotels on your own. They're a small chain, super easy."

"Is it too much to ask that I have my assistant with me to lend a helping hand?"

"Actually, yes, it is. I had much better things to do this week."

"Really? Things like what?"

"Grocery shopping, bill paying, napping—you know, those normal, boring things that non-rich people do."

I broke out in a laugh. "Oh, yeah. Okay. Now you're just being a smart-ass. I have bills too, you know? And I like naps just as much as the next person."

She fought a grin and looked out of the window. I scanned her as she sat in her yellow dress and sandals.

"You know why I really brought you with me. I wasn't kidding about Ariel. It's not serious with her. What I do with her is all for show."

"So, when the day comes that Ariel's father asks when you guys are getting married, then what?"

"Then...that's when I'll make an exit plan. I only need a couple more investments from him before I'll be okay without them. I owe a lot of people. Once that happens, I'll be done with Ariel for good."

"Interesting how you use people to get what you want. Do you always do that, Finn?"

I groaned and peered out of the window. "You're impossible, Quinn."

"Just saying."

"Anyway, when we get there, we'll have the meeting with Viking, and then I was thinking gambling and dinner."

"Jesus, Finn! Do you have to control every single thing, even down to plans? What if I want to—oh, I don't know—go for a walk or grab myself a drink or take a nap after the meeting?"

"I was just saying." I shifted in my seat. "Look, it's hard for me *not* to plan ahead, okay? If I don't, then I feel like I don't have my shit together. Perhaps it is a bit of a control issue, but I like things planned. It's just the way I'm wired."

"Well, look. We're going to Vegas, okay? Once the meeting is over, we'll have the rest of the day to do whatever we want. So let's just try and wing it? Have some fun with it, you know? Hell, you dragged me on this trip, the least you can do is let me have some fun."

"Okay, okay," I smiled, raising my hands in the air. "Fine. We can have some fun...however you want."

"See?" she sang. "Was that so hard?"

"Yeah, yeah, yeah. Zip it, Quinn."

CHAPTER TWENTY-ONE

RACHEL

When we landed in Vegas, Finn checked us into our hotel (separate rooms, this time), and then we grabbed a quick bite to eat from a café before going to Viking Hotel to meet with their team.

The meeting was short and swift, and of course, Finn was on top of the deal. He was as smart as a whip and a great speaker. I could always see through his bullshit, but if I were a total stranger and he was a salesman trying to sell lollipops on the street, I was sure he'd swindle me into buying a dozen. He was that smooth.

After the meeting, we went to the mall, where Finn allowed me to shop while he trailed behind.

"I'm not used to this, Quinn," he muttered.

"Well, get over it, bucko."

"Does strolling around in a store and browsing through all the clothes on the rack really make women happy? Is that what really brings women joy and makes them feel like they're in heaven?" he asked sarcastically.

"Oh, yes. Like you wouldn't believe!" I said, tossing in my own whopping of sarcasm.

"How does it not get boring?"

"Because the stores are always adding new styles, designs—keeps the ladies entertained." I grabbed a shimmery silver dress from the rack. "Maybe I should wear this while we gamble. Might bring us good luck."

"Hmm...no." He stepped forward and plucked the gold dress from the rack. "Gold would look much better on you. Plus, gold is worth more than silver."

"Okay." I fought a smile.

He placed the dress over his arm. "I'm buying. Pick out whatever you want."

"Are you serious?" I guffawed.

"Go shop, Quinn. Before I change my mind."

I brought a hand to my mouth to cover my smile,

but my hand didn't stay there for long. He reached up and pulled it away from my mouth.

"Why do you hide your smile?" he asked.

"I'm not hiding."

"Your smile is fucking gorgeous, Rachel." Our eyes locked, his shimmering beneath the lights. "Don't hide it from me. I love knowing that I make you smile. Proves you don't fully hate me."

Okay. This time I couldn't *not* smile. A full-blown grin swept across my face. Gah, what was this man doing to me? He was my boss. He was fucking Finn, for Christ's sake. I thought I couldn't stand him but his words...his actions. Ugh. He was making my cold heart melt.

"Anyway." I cleared my throat and grabbed the dress hanging off his arm. "You're practically giving me an unlimited shopping budget, so I'm going to take advantage of it and make you regret your decision later."

He smiled. "You have fifteen minutes."

"Fifteen? Are you kidding?" I screeched. "That's the amount of time it takes just for me to try clothes on!"

"Chop, chop!" He clapped his hands twice rapidly. "Better get to it then, Quinn!"

"I knew the asshole was still in there somewhere," I countered, sticking my tongue out.

I heard him laugh as I wandered down the aisle, suddenly feeling competitive to find as many clothes as I wanted, try them all on, and purchase most of it before his measly fifteen minutes were over.

CHAPTER TWENTY-TWO

FINN

I'd been to Vegas multiple times and gambled a lot, but being there with Rachel was a completely different experience.

She was fun, whether she cared to admit it or not. She thought she could fool me with her serious façade, but I was having the most amazing time with her...and it felt weird as fuck.

I wasn't used to whatever this feeling was. I looked at her beneath all the bright lights and glittery chandeliers, and my heart did weird spasms in my chest. Whenever I saw her talk or sip her drink, I wanted to steal every kiss from her plump lips. And when guys would stare or hit on her, it made me want to punch them in the face. I'd had several instances where I'd stand closer to her just to get them to back the hell off.

I thought about that night we had together in the hotel when we called our truce. How she drove me crazy with her body, made me feel like a man. Made me feel vulnerable for the first time ever with a woman.

It felt like forever since that night, our connection had become stronger, and no, it wasn't just the sex. It was something more–something I couldn't quite place my finger on.

At first, I couldn't stand the woman in front of me, but now I couldn't imagine what it would've been like without her around. She'd become an asset at the office as well as in my personal life, and I wanted to keep her around–hang onto that feeling.

"What are you thinking about?" Rachel asked, pulling the lever of her slot machine down.

I sighed, reaching for my lever too. "Just...stuff."

"Seems like some pretty deep stuff. Your face is all twisted up like you're upset about something."

I looked over and expected her to already be looking at me, but she was focused on the machine, crossing her fingers and hoping for a win.

"You wanna get out of here?"

Her head turned, and she met my eyes. "Sure. We can go. Are you okay?"

"Yeah. I just want to go someplace quieter. Have a drink to wind down or something. I think waking up early is starting to catch up with me."

"Well, we can go back to my room or yours if you want to," she shrugged.

"I'd like that."

We collected our things and made our way to the elevator. When we stepped inside, she stood across from me, pressing the button for our floor. It was only us on the elevator, which had been a first since arriving.

As the elevator ascended, she found my eyes and forced a smile. "You sure you're okay?"

"Yeah. I'm okay."

"You're acting all weird."

I took a step toward her. "Rachel."

"Hmm?"

"Tell me you don't feel this too."

"Feel what?" she asked, standing a little taller and bringing her clutch closer to her chest.

"*This*. What we have. There's a connection between us. I know you feel it."

"Finn..." She shook her head and looked at the glowing buttons of the elevator.

"All day I've been feeling this strong pull towards you..."

"That's just because we came here together. We've been drinking. And it's just sex. You want sex again, and that's fine."

"No—it's not just that. I'd know if it was just sex, but it's not." I was closing her in now.

She tipped her chin and looked up into my eyes. "Finn...don't."

"Don't what?"

"Don't try and make this into something we both know it shouldn't be."

"What do you mean?"

"I mean...well, we'd never work, and you know it."

"Says who?"

"Says the world. Every sign screams for me to stay away from you—to not take you seriously. To just have fun with whatever it is we have and then when it's time to let go, to let it go."

"Well, I don't feel that." I brought a hand up and clasped her chin between the tips of my fingers.

"What do you feel?"

"I feel something deeper for you. Something

stronger than whatever bullshit you try to tell yourself."

"I'm complicated," she murmured.

"So am I."

"It wouldn't be fair to Katie or Aaron."

"Are you kidding me?" I scoffed. "I love them, but fuck them right now. They're happy. Why can't we be happy too?"

"Okay. Fair point, but what about Ariel?" she countered quickly.

"I told you. Only a few more investments, Quinn."

"And how long will that take?"

"I don't know...a couple of months at least."

"So, you want me to wait a couple of months for you to pretend you're not already in a relationship."

I worked hard to swallow. "Don't make it sound so horrible."

"It is horrible, Finn. I can only see this blowing up in your face if her father finds out you're fucking another woman behind his daughter's back. I mean... imagine you meet someone from work who knows him personally. They see us together and tell him. Then you're fucked, your company might be at risk, and then you'd take it out on me. You'd resent me for *your* screw-up because that's what you do best. You're a master at resenting me."

The elevator chimed, and the doors drew apart. We'd reached our floor, and Rachel walked out, huffing and flustered, but we weren't done with this conversation yet.

"I have never resented you, Rachel," I called after her, but she kept marching in her heels to get to the end of the hallway where her room was.

"Let's just call this night off. We should both get some sleep anyway," she muttered over her shoulder. She approached her door, pulling out her keycard. As she stuck it in, I reached her and spun her around to face me.

"You're the one who resented me. You're the one who has continued to bring Ariel up, but you know she's not the real issue."

"What are you talking about?" I saw her throat bob up and down, her eyes suddenly looking everywhere else but at me.

"You know Ariel isn't the issue. You're just using her as an excuse because you're afraid. You're worried I'm going to hurt you. You want me to resent you because resenting you would be much easier for you to accept instead of the truth."

"What truth?" she breathed.

"That I love you...and you love me. And you can't deny it. We've known each other for years, we've felt this pull for as long as we've met each other. We mesh, Rachel. We're fucking *fire* together, and you know if we took this further, we'd be great together. But you're afraid...and you're trying to use any excuse to find a way out."

She waved a dismissive hand and turned away, twisting the doorknob to go into the suite. "Goodnight, Finn."

I held onto her arm. "Rachel."

"Finn—please. I'm not doing this!" Her head shook rapidly. I could tell she wanted to cry, but that wasn't the reason I brought this conversation to play. I cupped her face in my hands and dropped my lips on hers. I kissed her slowly, carefully. She whimpered and then moaned, kissing me right back.

Her palm pressed flat on my chest when our lips parted, and she said, "Why do you always have to be right?"

I smiled down at her, and it was enough to go for more. I kissed her again, backing her into the room. The door clicked shut behind us, and I picked her up in my arms, carrying her to the bed. Laying her down gently, I climbed on top of her and continued kissing her soft lips. I'd wanted to kiss her all night, and it was happening. Her mouth was on mine, our bodies connected.

She sighed as I dragged my lips to the arch of her neck.

"Finn," she breathed as I slid a palm up her bare thigh.

"I don't want you to deny me anymore, Rachel. Let me have you. I want you to be mine."

She moaned as I lowered my head, kissing the insides of her thighs. I shoved the hem of her dress up, bringing the kisses higher, higher, until my lips found her thong.

I licked the fabric, sucked it, kissed it until it was damp—until she was wet and writhing—and with a finger, I eventually slid her panties aside and ate her pussy. She tasted good, fresh. And I could tell her pussy was eager for me. I rolled my tongue over her clit, slid it through the lips. I repeated my actions over and over again until her hand was in my hair, gripping and squeezing, while she came.

"Oh, Finn!" she cried.

She released my hair slowly, and I sat up, unbuckling my belt and undoing my pants. Once my briefs were gone, I grabbed her hand and lifted her up.

"Ride me," I commanded.

"Kay."

I rested my back against the headboard, and she slowly sank down on my cock. Her pussy wrapped around me, tight and slick, and my body grew tense, already on the verge of coming.

"*Fuck*, Rachel."

She held my shoulders and rocked her hips, moving them forward and backward. I held her waist as she lifted up and down, her hair falling in her face, her pink nipples close to my lips. I leaned forward and sucked her nipple, and she moaned, riding me harder, faster.

"Fuck, I love you," I sighed. "I love this so much."

"Oh, Finn." She wrapped her arms around my neck, grinding on my cock until I groaned, and before I knew it, I was coming inside her.

"Damn, Rach!"

I went still, my cock throbbing as I released. Every drop was in her, and something about that made me feel like a king.

When I was no longer throbbing, she leaned back and looked me in the eyes.

"I love you too," she murmured. "But I swear to God if you hurt me, Finn, I'm going to punch you in your fucking throat."

"Fair enough," I said, and we both laughed.

She climbed off, and we showered. We had sex again in there, her hand pressed to the glass wall while I fucked her from behind, clutching a handful of her hair.

After the shower, we ordered room service and had a couple of drinks from the minibar, and while we ate, we talked about more activities we could do in Vegas the next day and even a few upcoming trips for work that we could make into getaways.

It was the perfect night with her. She was so relaxed, so comfortable and open with me. She was glowing, and I'd never seen her like this before. So angelic. So happy. It was a sight to behold, and I was glad to be the one who made it happen.

This night with her was everything...

But then the next morning happened, and it ruined everything.

CHAPTER TWENTY-THREE

RACHEL

Once again, waking up in Finn's arms was a dream. The sun was slowly peeking over the horizon, and Vegas life was already calling to me at eight in the morning. My belly grumbled as I thought about breakfast, and then I heard Finn laugh.

"What's so funny?" I asked, smiling.

"You're always hungry."

"I am not!"

"You so are. No shame in that. I'm hungry too."

I sat up on one elbow and looked out of the window. "I am hungry, but seriously, look at this view. I could wake up here every morning."

Finn sat up with me. "Yeah."

"Breakfast?" I asked.

"Definitely." I climbed out of bed as he said, "I'll just go over to my room to change."

"Okay. Meet me back here."

Finn went to his room next door, and when the door shut behind him, I went for my suitcase to find something to wear. I decided to go with a pair of jean shorts and a silk blouse.

After putting in my earrings and completing my final touches, I picked up my phone and took a picture of my view. Because seriously, I needed to remember my spent time there.

I waited for Finn, but when thirty minutes passed, and he still hadn't shown up, I got worried.

I sent him a text.

Everything ok?

I waited a few minutes for him to respond, but he didn't. I figured he must've been showering, shaving, or something, so I grabbed my purse and key card and left my room to go to his. I gave his door a rapid knock, and it was answered immediately.

Only it wasn't Finn who'd answered.

It was a woman.

CHAPTER TWENTY-FOUR

RACHEL

"Hi! You must be Rachel, Finn's assistant, right? Finn's told me all about you! I'm Ariel!" Ariel stood on the other side of the door, her hair dark-brown all the way down her back and her skin naturally tan. She had on a face full of makeup and wore a peach-colored dress with sandals.

I hesitated a moment, unsure what to say. "I —I am."

I heard steps, and Finn was hurrying to the door. When his eyes met mine, instant regret pooled in them.

"Are you guys going somewhere?" she asked.

"You look really nice, Rachel. Is there a meeting or something?"

What the hell is she doing here?

"I was just taking Rachel to breakfast to celebrate yesterday's successful closing," Finn said, looking at me, hoping I'd go along.

"Oh, babe! You closed?" she squealed, then she threw her arms around his neck and bounced up and down in his arms. All I could see were her breasts rubbing up and down on his chest. The chest I was just laying my head on last night.

I looked away, feeling a familiar tightening in my chest that I didn't like.

"Is it okay if I come too?" she asked when she let him go.

"Um...actually, I have a few work things to discuss with Rachel, Ariel."

"That's okay. I'll be quiet, I promise." She pretended to zip her lips and toss the key.

Finn and I locked eyes, and I wanted to scream. Screw this. What the fuck was she doing in Vegas? Did he tell her to come?

"Kay," Finn sighed.

"Yay! Let me get my bag. BRB, babe!"

When Ariel had rounded the corner, I stepped

forward. "Are you fucking *kidding* me? Why is she here, Finn?"

"I don't know! She knocked on the fucking door an hour ago, and I've been trying to get her to leave since!"

"Did you tell her you were here?"

"No. Apparently, she told Audrey she wanted to surprise me, and Audrey told her where I was. Gave her my room number and everything."

"Wow." I shook my head. "There's no way I'm going to breakfast with you two."

"Yes, you will. After breakfast, I'll get rid of her. I promise."

"Ready!" Ariel sang, popping up next to Finn again. I moved away from the door and turned away, marching toward the elevator.

Inside the elevator, Ariel was closer to Finn than ever, her arm wrapped in his, her head on his shoulder. It was hard not to see them, and everything inside me burned and wept.

Eating with them was much worse. Ariel talked all about the trips they took together and even mentioned how they should have gotten hitched in Vegas just to show her dad that they did love each other. Finn didn't say much, just focused on his food.

When Ariel excused herself to go to the restroom, I picked up my purse.

"I can't do this, Finn."

"Rachel, please," he pleaded. "I'll get rid of her, I swear."

"It doesn't look like she's going anywhere anytime soon, Finn!"

"Can you keep your voice down, please?"

"Why? So she doesn't overhear and tell her rich daddy on you? You know what, Finn? This is fucking pathetic. It's honestly useless. She came here to surprise you, and she's clearly not going to leave anytime soon, so I will." I shoved back in my chair.

Finn came out right after me, catching me by the elbow. "Rachel, please don't leave."

"I *have* to go," I said, shrugging him off. And when I left the restaurant, I didn't look back, no matter how much it killed me not to.

CHAPTER TWENTY-FIVE

FINN

It took four hours after Rachel left to get rid of Ariel. She wanted to gamble, go to dispensaries, and take pictures for her Instagram. I finally faked a call and told her I had an urgent meeting with Viking Hotels and wasn't sure how long it would last because they also wanted to golf. She took the bait, which I knew she would, despite the fact that I hated golfing. Ariel didn't know that, though. She didn't know shit about anyone but herself.

When Ariel was gone, that only left one thing for me to do. I left my room and walked over to Rachel's.

"Please still be here," I pleaded while knocking.

And I waited.

And waited. There was no response.

I took out the extra key card to her room and stuck it in. But I should've known when I opened the door, she wasn't going to be there, and neither would her things. The room was completely vacant, the bed properly made, and the closets and dressers clear.

Just like that, she was gone...and we were back to square one.

Back to Rachel Quinn hating me all over again.

CHAPTER TWENTY-SIX

FINN

I wasn't sure what to expect Monday morning at the office, but I'd hoped Rachel would be there. She hadn't answered or returned any of my calls after I checked her hotel room and found it empty.

And seeing as I had her address information from work, I was tempted to visit her, but I didn't want to be that asshole who showed up unannounced, only to be demonized even more by a woman who already hated my guts.

So, I waited, and the waiting was pure torture.

But that morning, I got ready per usual and headed to the office, cruising in my Mercedes G-

Class while thinking about all the ways I could get her to forgive me.

I told her I loved her, for Christ's sake. I had *never* done that before. There was no way I could just let her walk away. For once, I was going to have to lower my guard and show her the real me, and that terrified me.

I parked in the private parking deck and took the VIP elevator up to the top floor. As soon as I stepped out, I noticed Audrey wasn't sitting at her desk, which wasn't normal for her on a Monday morning.

Ignoring the thought, I went to my office, but not without looking for Rachel at her desk. She wasn't there either.

As I peeled out of my suit jacket and placed my briefcase on the desk, there was a small knock at the door behind me. I turned around, and Audrey was there, her lips pressed flat and a desolate look in her eyes.

"Good morning, Audrey," I said. "Everything okay?"

"Yes, everything's fine. Well...um, not really. I received an email this morning. From Rachel."

My heart started being faster, but I remained cool and slid the tips of my fingers into my front pockets. "Okay..."

"She doesn't want to come into work anymore. For personal reasons, I suppose. She said she left her two-weeks' notice on your desk, but if she has to, she is willing to fulfill her time here for the two weeks remaining."

"Uh...no. It's fine," I murmured. "She doesn't have to come in anymore if she doesn't want to. But count her hours for the next two weeks and make sure she's paid for them."

"Sir. Are you sure?"

"Yes, Audrey. I'm sure. Just do it."

Audrey nodded and looked away. "Okay." She turned away and walked out of the office, and as if she'd sensed that I needed a moment alone, she closed the door behind her. Audrey was the type to always ask whether someone wanted the door open or closed. Not today, and it made me wonder if she'd known something was sparking between Rachel and me too. She knew we'd gone to Vegas together. She sent Ariel my way—not purposely—but it happened, and perhaps she knew something had gone terribly wrong between Rachel and me in Vegas, thus proving it to be true to her.

Man. This wasn't good.

CHAPTER TWENTY-SEVEN

RACHEL

"Am I just being a selfish bitch?" I whined into the phone. Pam was on the other line, working per usual, and it felt just like it had a couple of weeks ago. Only, this time I had hope.

I'd quit working for Finn. I had to. There was no way I could face him after what'd happened in Vegas —after he'd told me he *loved* me. And I was so ready and willing to give myself to him—give him all of me, despite how terrified I was. I was glad I didn't because just when I thought we were safe, in came a tornado to sweep it all away. It was probably better this way anyway.

Fortunately, I'd gotten an email for an interview with a local publicity company, which excited me. It was a smaller company, but they had great range.

"No, you're not being selfish, Rach. Honestly, if you ask me, he's the one being selfish. I mean, he's literally using some girl so he can continue having his company invested in. He sounds like a prick."

"Yeah, he is a prick. But...ugh, Pam, he was *my* prick. And for a moment, I thought we could be something, but then *she* showed up. And I don't even blame her. I mean, how could I? She has no clue we're sleeping together. No one does—well, except you now."

"Wait. You haven't told Katie about this?"

"God, no. Katie would beg me to make things right so that whenever we're both around each other again, we're decent to each other. She hates seeing us fight. And the last time I spoke to her, we were getting along."

"Right. And you're really not going to work for him anymore?"

"I can't, Pam. I have to keep my dignity. I can't let him think it's okay shoving her in my face just because she wants to surprise him. I have standards and morals, okay? And they're not about to disappear for him."

Pam stopped typing, which made me think she was thinking. "You want to know what I think?"

Yep. I was right. She was thinking. "What?"

"I think you're putting barbed wire around your heart, Rach."

"I am not!" I shouted, springing up on my bed.

"Yes, you are. And it's because of that dumbass ex of yours, Marco. Look, is this Finn guy perfect? No, I'm sure he's not, but what guy is? He told you he loved you, and you even admitted that you don't think he hands those words out to just any woman. He feels something for you. He's been calling you nonstop, and you respond with a two-weeks' notice? I don't want to make excuses for the man, but the least you can do is let him try and make things right. Let him work for it. Yes, he should grovel, but hell... let him do it. It'll prove how much he really wants you."

I shook my head. "I can't face him again, Pam. I just can't. Not right now."

"What if Aaron or Katie have an event, and he's there?"

"Then...I'll avoid him."

"I highly doubt he'll avoid you, though," she responded arrogantly.

I sighed. "This is crazy. I can't believe I'm even giving him so much thought."

"It's because you love him too, Rach. I've seen love on you—I've heard it. You were falling for him."

I chewed on the corner of my bottom lip, feeling the urge to cry. God, Pam was right. She was so, so right. I was falling for Finn. He was opening up to me, and I was lowering my guard, and we were great together when we weren't arguing or biting each other's heads off.

But Ariel. He clearly needed her more than he needed me, and that didn't look like it would be changing anytime soon. I refused to be a woman in the middle.

As if Pam had read my mind, she said, "Takes two to tango, sister."

"Ugh. Bye, Pam. You're not helping."

She laughed, and we ended the call, and I flopped back on my bed, squeezing my eyes shut, unable to get Finn's green eyes off my mind.

CHAPTER TWENTY-EIGHT

FINN

It was a slow night at Brotherhood. Then again, it was a Tuesday, and not many men bothered coming on weekdays due to their busy schedules.

I couldn't stand being at work a second longer. The second day without Rachel was even harder than the first. Her desk was still there, along with her cups and notebooks and one of the pink mugs she always drank coffee in.

All that day, I kept hoping she'd show up, maybe to clear her desk or give me an official notice in person, but she didn't. And she wouldn't. She'd let me throw it all and burn it before coming back to Brewer to face me.

"So, you actually slept with her?" Jake asked, leaning back and looking at me. "I fucking knew it, man! I knew you were attracted to her! I knew your whole *I don't sleep with my employee's* motto was complete bullshit!"

I waved the finger he was pointing at me away. "Yeah, yeah."

"You've fucked up. You know that?" Jake asked, then chugged down an ample amount of beer. "She hates your ass. But hey, who's to say you can't meet up for a final hate-fuck?"

"No, Jake. It's not like that, okay?" I rubbed my forehead. "I told you about the night we spent together, but there was more to it. I told her some serious shit."

"Serious shit like what?"

"I told her I *loved* her."

Jake froze a moment, and I didn't have to look at him to know he was staring a hole into the side of my head. "Well, shit, man. Do you?"

"Yeah–I mean, I think so. I don't know. She does shit to me, man. She drives me crazy, and I think about her nonstop. When we're together, everything is so effortless."

"Holy shit. Sounds like you really *do* love her."

"I've been thinking about going to her apartment to get her to talk to me. She won't answer my calls or texts. I don't know what else to do."

"Well, the woman who you claim isn't your girlfriend, yet everyone else thinks she is, did show up the night after you two fucked each other's brains out, so I'm pretty sure that warrants blocked phone calls."

I scowled at him. "You are literally not fucking helping."

Jake tossed his hands up and laughed. "Okay, okay. I know this is serious. I'll stop fucking around."

"Please," I grumbled before sipping my beer. It had to be beer tonight–something light and easy. Anything too heavy was going to make me lose my mind.

"Do you want my honest opinion?" Jake asked after a while.

"Yes."

"You can't show up at her place. If she gave your secretary a two-weeks' notice and hasn't shown up to work, she's done, man. If she still wanted a chance at it, she'd have made an appearance by now."

"But Rachel is stubborn," I countered.

"Doesn't matter. If she really, really wanted to

make it work with you, she would've shown her face by now. It's just how women operate. They need that sort of closure."

I lowered my head, staring at the label on my beer bottle. "I have *never* told a woman I love her. Only my mother. Nobody else. If I shouldn't show up at her place, what the fuck should I do then?"

Jake shrugged. "That's the hard part, brother," he said, clapping my shoulder. "You could go see her, but she can also ignore you. Or...you can allow some time to pass and for her emotions to settle before making a move. Maybe even clean up your shit with Ariel and Rich Daddy so you can prove to her that you did it all to be with her." Jake downed the rest of his drink. "Just my opinion."

"Damn, Jake. When did you become a love doctor?"

He tossed his head back and laughed. "Trust me, I'm no love doctor. Don't have time for that shit."

"But weren't you just telling me about some new intern you were thinking about sleeping with?" I mused.

"Okay...that's a different story. I *will* sleep with her. It's just...well, our circumstances are a little weird. And she's kind of stubborn. But I can tell she sees me, ya know? I look at her, and she looks at me, and we *see* each other. Sometimes I catch myself staring at her without her realizing it."

"Sounds creepy, Jake."

He shrugged. "She smiles back."

"Yeah, probably because you're her boss, and she doesn't want to offend you."

Jake mulled that over. "Hmm...well, when you put it that way..."

I huffed a laugh as he went on about how nerdy the intern was, but also how he couldn't stop hearing her out on many of her ideas. He definitely wanted her, but the more he described her as being stubborn and not caving to him, the more she reminded me of Rachel.

Jake was right.

I had to clean up my shit first if I wanted Rachel back.

CHAPTER TWENTY-NINE

RACHEL

Katie called and told me she was having a last-minute surprise party for Aaron's birthday, and I was dreading it. I should've had this date marked on my calendar because anything that involved Aaron also included Finn.

I wanted to make up an excuse, tell her I was working or sick, but before I could, she told me she was going to need my help with decorating and setting up. And who was I to deny my bestie a helping hand? Katie loved Aaron, and just because I didn't want to see Finn didn't mean I needed to take it out on her.

According to Katie, it was Finn's job to make sure Aaron was with him while all the guests gathered. I figured as soon as we all screamed our surprises, then I could bail while Aaron and Finn weeded their way through the crowd. Katie's house was big enough. I was sure I could sneak out without being noticed.

As I walked out of the PR office and into the busy streets of LA, Katie was waiting for me in front of the building.

"Come on! Get in! We only have six hours to get all the shit for the party and decorate, and you know LA traffic is a bitch!"

I climbed into the car and placed my purse on my lap after buckling in. "Are we the only two setting up?" I asked.

"No, Ally is also helping. And we don't have to worry about food or drinks because I hired a caterer for that. I just want tonight to be perfect. Aaron has been working so hard, and he deserves this. And speaking of, I heard Finn just landed a huge deal with Viking Hotels!"

"Yeah, I heard too." I peered out of the window. I couldn't look at Katie while she spoke of Finn, and, fortunately, she was more concerned about Aaron's surprise than whatever I was feeling. I'd heard Finn scored a bigger deal with Viking, which had obviously happened after I left. I wasn't sure if he'd renegotiated or what, but apparently, he'd signed for seven years with their company, which resulted in a multi-million-dollar deal. All that money...and I still couldn't figure out why he needed Ariel and her father. Was it because he felt indebted to her? Was he worried her father would smear his name and reputation? It didn't make any sense. Finn was perfectly capable on his own, and the fact that he hadn't gotten rid of Ariel yet only proved to me that he still had feelings for her and wasn't completely ready to let her go. Then again, it's been several days now, and I didn't know what his status with Ariel was anymore.

Still, she was all over him in Vegas, and he didn't seem too put off by it. He kept giving me his sympathy glances, but it wasn't like he was shoving her away or telling her to stop. He just allowed her to do it...all while I stood or sat right beside them. What girl deserved that sort of treatment right after being told she was loved?

Katie and I spent the day picking up everything and even made a quick stop for her to buy a dress. Apparently, the hundreds of dresses in her closet weren't good enough. Four hours later and we were at Katie and Aaron's mansion.

I loaded my hands and arms with bags from the trunk and lugged them into the house, and we got straight to work, moving around the caterers and DJ booth to decorate.

When we were done, we put on makeup, got dressed, and before I knew it, the sun was setting, guests had filled up the living room and were mingling with drinks in hand, and Katie had received a text from Finn, alerting her that he was on the way with Aaron.

I sighed at the thought of Finn. I had to bolt as soon as he walked through that door. I was going to tell Katie I wasn't feeling well or that I had late-night work to do for the agency—anything if it meant getting away from the party and as far away from Finn as possible.

"Okay, guys! Shh! He's here! He's here!" Katie hissed minutes later. "He's pulling into the driveway right now. Ally, get the lights!"

Ally rushed to the light switches and turned them off, and then everyone crouched, smiling eagerly as they waited for the birthday boy.

I lowered to a squat next to Katie by the sofa, and she giggled while looking at me. "He's going to be so surprised.

God. She was so happy. I needed to tell her that I

had to go and why. I didn't want to ruin her night by just disappearing without explanation. She was my best friend.

"Katie...I need to tell you something."

"Yeah, babe. Of course—but can it wait just five minutes?" She lifted her head and looked out of the window. "They're coming up the sidewalk."

"Yeah, of course." I forced a smile at her and then peered through the curtain. I saw Aaron coming up first, talking about how badly he needed a drink. And trailing right behind him was Finn. My heart lurched in my chest. I looked away, down at the purple nail polish on my fingernails.

"Okay, guys, get ready!" Katie whisper hissed.

The lock on the door clicked, and Aaron's voice was much clearer as he loudly wondered where Katie was and why it was so dark inside the house if her car was there.

When the door swung open, and Aaron switched on a light, everyone sprung up and yelled SURPRISE! I shouted it too, but my smile immediately faded when my eyes shifted to the man behind him.

Finn.

As if I was the first person he was looking for, his

eyes locked right on mine, and all I could make out was guilt.

I pulled my gaze away and forced a smile at Katie and Aaron as they hugged and kissed. Aaron exclaimed how insanely surprised he was and gave Katie another kiss, and then some of the guests approached, and this felt like the right time to leave, so I turned away and went to the kitchen to get my purse. It took everything in me not to look back at Finn.

I collected my purse from the top of the fridge and hurried for the double doors that lead out to the pool. There was a gate and a path I could take to get to the front of the house. I'd call an Uber and wait at the curb if I had to. Text Katie and tell her I wasn't feeling well—I didn't care. I just couldn't be in the same room as Finn right now.

Just as I stepped outside, I heard footsteps behind me.

"Rachel," a deep voice called after me.

I worked hard to swallow but kept going. I rounded the pool, and he called my name even louder.

"Rachel, please!" he called. I heard the door shut behind him and came to an abrupt halt. My breaths came out slow, shallow as I heard his steps coming closer and closer. "Rachel, I need to talk to you."

I turned around. "There's nothing to talk about, Finn."

"Why are you leaving?" he asked.

"I'm not feeling well," I lied.

"You look fine to me."

"Yeah, well, seeing certain people makes me sick to my stomach sometimes."

Finn's eyes stretched, and then he pressed his lips and nodded. "Okay. I guess I deserve that one." He took two steps closer. I took one back.

"What do you want?"

"I landed a great deal with Viking," he said.

"I saw. Are you here to brag?"

"No. I just wanted to tell you that the articles aren't accurate. Viking originally wanted a two-year deal, remember? I fought for the seven years after you left Vegas."

I narrowed my eyes. "I don't understand..."

"I fought for the seven years to get enough money to cover any future investments I would need from Ariel's father and to pay back everyone I owed." Another step closer. This time I didn't move. "Rachel... I—" Finn clamped his mouth shut, and my next breath came out soft. "I can't be without you, okay? I fought tooth and nail for this deal because I wanted to make things right and because I wanted you. Only you, okay? And yes, I know I'm a jackass for stringing Ariel along. I know I'm a fucking shit-head for using her and her dad to build my company, but... I was doing what I had to do to stay afloat. But you made me realize that things like that...they won't get me far. Especially when it comes to being one hundred percent open to someone else."

He was standing right in front of me now, his eyes trained on mine. "Finn..."

"I love you, Rachel Quinn. And I want to be with you. I want you back. I think about you every night. I toss and turn and hope like hell you don't hate me. I know I messed up...I just didn't think it would backfire like this. I didn't think my heart would get so involved. But it beats for you, Rachel. And I don't give a damn how much you despise me or how badly you want to slap the shit out of me, it will always beat for you."

My eyes had filled to the brim with tears, and my heart was beating so hard I could hear my pulse in my ears. I had never, ever been spoken to like this—so passionately, so raw and honest.

I felt the gaping hole in my chest healing with every word but also aching because everything he was saying was genuine. It was all I wanted to hear, but I was so hurt and guarded that I didn't want to give him the chance. Really, I didn't want to give anyone the chance of hurting me anymore. But I had hurt him too. I guess we were even in that way.

"Finn, I—"

He lifted a hand and cupped my cheek. "Quinn...I need you."

"I know. You said that, but...I can't."

"Why can't you?"

"Because I'm scared you'll hurt me again, okay?"

This time he cradled my face in both his hands and forced me to look at him. "Rachel—I will *never, ever* hurt you again, do you hear me? I'm sorry for what happened in Vegas. I'm sorry for the way you were treated, but I swear to you I will never hurt you like I did in Vegas."

I closed my eyes, and tears dripped down my cheeks, but I nodded. "Okay," I whispered. Then I wiped my eyes and looked up at him. "Okay," I repeated firmly. "And you swear no more Ariel? Ever?"

"I swear. No more Ariel. No more of her dad. I'm much better off without them." His eyes lit up, and he smiled. "Wow...who knew I could make

Rachel Quinn cry? And all this time, I thought your soul was made of black matter."

"Oh, shut up," I laughed, and he laughed too before reeling me in and kissing me. And this wasn't like the kisses we'd shared before. This one was passionate and measured and slow as if he'd been waiting for this kiss to happen for a very long time and wanted to savor every second of it.

Hell, I'd wanted the same. And now I had it. *We* had it.

I heard a door shut, and then someone called my name. "Rachel?"

I pulled away from Finn and looked in the direction of the voice. Katie was coming down the stone steps and toward the pool area in her heels. "Oh my God! Were you two just *kissing*?" she screeched.

Finn and I looked at each other before laughing, and I started to answer, but Katie shook her head and said, "No! Don't even say anything! I saw it! I came looking for you, and I found you kissing *Finn*! Hell must be freezing or something!"

I laughed, and Finn wrapped an arm around me. "Katie...you have no issue with us wanting to be together, do you?"

"What? No! Why would I have an issue with it? I like you, Finn, and of course, I love Rachel and want to see her happy. Oh my god, babe. Was this what you wanted to talk to me about? I'm so sorry I told you to wait!"

"No, no! It wasn't this—well, it *was* this, but not the happiest version of it." I winced and looked at Finn. "No offense."

Finn shrugged. "None taken."

"Aww!" Katie clasped her hands together. "I'm so happy for you guys! Finally, you two can stop fighting each other and love each other!"

The back door to the house opened again, and out came Aaron with a beer in hand. "Oh, hey! Wait—Rachel, you're actually letting Finn *touch* you?"

I laughed and held onto Finn's hand that was around my shoulder.

"Babe! They're dating!" Katie chimed.

"What? Holy shit, congrats! See, Katie Kat, I told you they were secretly having sex."

"What?" I yelped.

"Aaron! You weren't supposed to bring that up!" Katie swatted at her husband.

"Well, they are, and we know it for a fact now, so it doesn't matter!" Aaron said, laughing. "Katie and I were talking one night about you working together, and I figured all the close proximity and hostility you two have would result in some...heated moments."

"It's totally like you to think something like that, Aaron," Finn said, chuckling.

"Hey, I know my best friend, alright? Women don't get under your skin the way Rachel does unless you're really into her. And Rachel? This dude was *really* into you and trying so hard to fight it."

I smiled up at Finn. "Well, I'm glad he's not fighting it anymore."

Finn looked down at me with nothing but love and joy in his green eyes. Then he turned me in his arms and kissed me again, and Aaron and Katie whooped and laughed, and I was so glad there wasn't anyone else outside they could embarrass us in front of.

Whether there were people around or not, though, this felt right. It felt real. And I wanted it to last forever.

EPILOGUE

FINN

Life felt much better now that I had Rachel. I was a happier man and never thought I'd see the day I settled down, yet there I was. I wrapped up on my last conference call before packing my work bag and leaving my office.

"Heading out, Mr. Weston?"

"I am, Audrey. I'll see you Monday."

"Have a great night!"

I took the elevator to the private parking deck and slid into my car, checking the time on my Versace watch before pulling out of the deck and heading downtown.

Once I'd reached my destination, I parked in front of the restaurant and climbed out, handing my keys to the valet. And when I entered, there she was.

My woman, Rachel Quinn. She was standing in the waiting area, dressed in a sleeveless gray dress and black heels. Her hair was pinned up, but several blonde tendrils hung around her face and at the nape of her neck. She turned her head when the door opened and when she spotted me, a wide, bright smile swept across her lips. I loved seeing her smile for the first time of any day. I loved knowing she looked forward to seeing me just as much as I did her.

"Hey, beautiful," I murmured in her ear, greeting her with a full hug and kiss. I hadn't seen her all week. She had to do work with her agency in New York for a few days. She'd left the previous company to start her own three months after we officially declared how much we wanted to be together, and her company had been soaring ever since.

She was great at her job and, seeing as everyone loved us as a couple, and we attended many events together now, it wasn't hard for her to win over a few of the big dogs so her company could flourish. I was positive that even without me, she would have found success.

"I missed you," she said, looking up at me. "Work is kicking our asses, huh?"

"It is, but it'll never stop me from being with the woman I love."

She laughed and held me around the neck. "Wow. Who knew Finn Weston could utter such romantic words?"

"What can I say? You bring out the romantic in me, babe."

She tossed her head back to laugh, and I kissed her throat. When the hostess called our names and sat us at our tables, I felt like the luckiest man alive. I was sitting across from the most beautiful woman I'd ever met, a woman I couldn't keep my eyes or hands off of.

I didn't think I would end up with someone like her. I thought we'd be enemies for life, always at each other's throats, but I was wrong. Turns out, we'd misunderstood one another. We had much more in common than I ever could have imagined, and I was glad to have found a partner in her.

Now, we were on the same page, and we were making the most of our love. There was no going back for me. Rachel Quinn was my one, and I was going to be hers forever.

THE END

ABOUT THE AUTHOR

Kylie King is a soccer mom by day, and a writer of ridiculously smutty romances by night. She loves reading, swimming, and mixed drinks that include lots of rum. All of her books are short and hot, with over-the-top fantasies that ALWAYS end with a romantic happily ever after.

For New Release Alerts & More:

Sign Up For Kylie King's Newsletter
at http://eepurl.com/cGBHij

or follow her on Instagram @authorkylieking

BOOKS BY KYLIE

You can find all of Kylie's books on Amazon and Free with Kindle Unlimited.
All are standalone novels that can be read in one sitting!

Serviced
Sweet Secrets
The Best Friend Hookup
Mister Baby Maker
Pleasing Her Prince
The Quarterback's Secret
Tempting Her Neighbor
My Arrogant Boss
Faking It With My Boss

www.ingramcontent.com/pod-product-compliance
Ingram Content Group UK Ltd.
Pitfield, Milton Keynes, MK11 3LW, UK
UKHW021649190726
13853UKWH00001B/149

9 798459 725988